STANTON, CALIFORNIA

D0556172

STANTON, CALIFORNIA

STORIES

SAM SILVAS

SILVER BIRCH PRESS
LOS ANGELES, CALIFORNIA

ISBN-13: 978-0692733202

ISBN-10: 0692733205

EMAIL: silver@silverbirchpress.com

WEB: silverbirchpress.com

BLOG: silverbirchpress.wordpress.com

MAILING ADDRESS:
Silver Birch Press
P.O. Box 29458
Los Angeles, CA 90029

"Building" originally appeared in *Chiron Review* (Spring 2006).

COVER PHOTO: "Misty river sunrise."

For Mom and Dad

Stories

THE UNLUCKIEST MAN
IN THE WORLD

I was raised to believe you made your own luck in this world. My dad and granddad were the two toughest men I ever knew, and they didn't want anything from anybody—not the government, the church, or another man. And anyone who knew them would say they turned out all right. My Uncle Wayne, my mom's brother, could've been like them, but spun himself out before he really got started.

I had every intention of following in their footsteps until a shit storm of bad luck rained down on me so hard and for so long I had no choice but to change my mind. Things hit me so square I still don't know if it's worth getting up every morning just so I can risk getting hit again. It took a lot to change my mind, but it was either change my mind or go crazy. I'll tell you my story and won't blame you if you don't believe it, but that doesn't mean it still isn't all true.

I grew up on the Sacramento Delta, too far from the city of Sacramento to say I was from there but not close enough to any other place else to say I wasn't from there. Houses hugged the river on both sides starting about twelve miles outside of the city. Every so often a cluster of houses would get together and call themselves a town, which usually consisted of a grocery store, a bar, a post office, and a restaurant just inland from the river. It was all volunteer fire departments, a doctor who still made house calls, and a sheriff instead of city police up and down my world.

The forty-mile stretch of the Sacramento River known as the Delta was different from any other part of it. It started two hundred miles to the north in Redding, spilling out of Shasta Lake, cold twenty feet down from the snow that slid off Mount Shasta. At its stem, it welcomed the Pit River from the east, a pattern it would repeat often on its journey to deliver itself to the San Francisco Bay. Along the way, it was the end of the line for the Feather River and the American River, both big enough on their own to appear on any map of California.

Flowing down Northern California, the Sacramento River carved out a wide presence through the unpopulated farmland of Tehema, Butte, and Sutter Counties, skirting towns that barely noticed its passing, other than to satisfy its irrigation needs. It carried enough water to make Southern California, Nevada, and Arizona both envious and desperate for it.

In Chico, the river was used only two weekends a year: On Labor Day and Memorial Day, students from the college filled the water with inner tubes and themselves with alcohol. The water was so slow moving and the river so wide-open that students could drink all day with the sun above them and the water underneath them and not have to worry about eddies or snags or anything that sniffed of being a rapid.

In the city of its surname, the river held tight to the western edge, hard by Old Town, its shore littered on either side with bars and restaurants for both tourists and locals. On summer weekends the river was full of ski and fishing boats, a perfect balance for what a man wanted and what a man needed.

Once the river left the city and made its way to where I lived, it narrowed and began twisting every fifty feet or so, as if bored with what it had been for all those previous miles and wanted to try something different. Tule grass and box elder and ash trees grew close to each other in the damp soil of the riverbank, with a few valley oak thrown in. The trees towered and curved over the water. At night, if not for the sound of the water, the river would seem to have disappeared in those trees. Most of the houses on the river were three- and four-generations old, passed down and lived in because no one ever thought to do anything else with them.

This section of the river was deemed so unworthy that a shipping channel was dug in 1963 to bypass it, and the Port of Sacramento was born. It begins in Sacramento and reattaches itself to the river in Suisan, just before entering the San Francisco Bay. The land I knew had been created by everything the river didn't or couldn't hold, layer after layer of sediment left behind to become tiny islands. The Delta had been here when the Indians lived on its banks, when the Spanish ran them off, and when Tule elk ate its vegetation before the flood of 1878 wiped them out. It would be here long after me and my family were gone. People outside the Delta thought the river served no purpose other than to irrigate the farmland that spread for miles around it. They were probably right, and that's why I loved it.

My granddad lived across the road from us in a little shack he inherited from his dad, and my mom's brother, who was antisocial because he had gotten syphilis from a whore in Vietnam and didn't get it treated in time, lived down river, which meant we either had to swim to him or spend money putting gas in our boat. Most everyone on the river owned an aluminum fishing boat with a small two-stroke engine not much bigger than those used on lawn mowers. No one bothered building a dock—when you visited someone, you just dragged your boat onto land and tied it to the nearest tree. All the men in my family did three things: We played football in high school, went into the service, and worked as glaziers after getting out.

Being a glass man wasn't bad as far as construction jobs went. It wasn't as hot as roof work, as dangerous as being a steel worker, or as messy as plumbing. Me, my brother, father, and grandfather were all colorblind. Not the kind where things were all grey, but the kind where you mix up yellow and green, so being electricians was out of the question. The work was indoors half the time, which was nice during the Sacramento summers where the land was so hard and flat it didn't absorb the heat but sent it right back up so it seemed like you were getting it from both ends. But once the sun slid behind the giant pines in the foothills that surrounded the Sacramento Valley, breezes that were so slight during the day as to barely ripple the river would gain strength and rush out of the Delta, carrying cool air for thirty miles in every direction. The entire valley was grateful for the evening breezes that made the days tolerable. When you told someone from Roseville or Folsom that you lived on the Delta, they would reply, Oh, thank god for those delta breezes, and act as if we had manufactured them or were responsible for them simply by living on the river. That was fine, it was nice to be known for something, but for us on

13

the Delta, those breezes were something even more, a signal that we had finally won the day, that we had outlasted the best the world could throw at us. I grew up believing I always would.

There was a glazier's union in downtown Sacramento but my family refused to join. Sure, the money and benefits were better than running your own crew but with our own company we didn't have to take shit from anyone and could work when we wanted to work and drink and fish when we wanted to drink and fish. Sacramento wasn't a strong union city like the Bay Area so there was always plenty of work, even if it meant having to drive all over the four counties that surrounded the city. Hell, being down on the Delta meant we were a half hour drive from anywhere, so what was another hour drive if you could make some money. Plus, more windshield time meant less time at home doing chores or having the old lady rag on you.

When I was about twelve, me and my brother swam down to my uncle's house to spend the night with him. Sometime in the middle of the night a woman showed up and stayed until morning. From our sleeping bags in the living room, we heard her complaining that our uncle never took her dancing or into Sacramento to a fancy restaurant. It was quiet for a while after all her talking, then my uncle simply said, "You can be replaced, you know." I've always remembered that day for two reasons: one, she ran her car key alongside his El Camino as she left, and a few days later little Scotty Oswald drowned in the river and my mom wouldn't let us swim down to my uncle's anymore. We pleaded with her to let us keep swimming but she wouldn't change her mind. It was the summer before my seventh-grade year and I was almost the height I am now, and was easily the strongest kid in my class. I didn't look like anything special with my shirt off, and still don't, but I haven't found many things I can't push and shove and lift once I set my mind to it. My brother was two years younger and not nearly as big, but he had plenty of fat on him to keep him afloat.

"Little Scotty didn't weigh more than sixty pounds," I said to my mom. "It's a miracle he didn't get swept away before."

14

"The Oswalds all have webbed feet," my mother replied. "That's a known fact. Right between the pinkie toe and the one next to it, whatever that one's called. If they can't swim without drowning, what chance do you have?"

My first piece of bad luck came my way through my baby brother. I had just come home from the Army and was spending my time—and all my money—drinking and playing low ball at Fred's. It was the only bar in town and was technically called Fred's on the River but no one called it that. I mean, we lived on the river, what the hell else could it be called? I swear, sometimes I think people are so dumb it's a wonder they know where to stick it long enough to keep the species going.

Fred was a friend of my dad's and even though I wasn't twenty-one yet would let me drink at the bar on weekdays as long as I didn't start any trouble. Years ago when the bar was called The Weeping Willow, the husband of a woman he was seeing on the sly cold-cocked him and dragged him outside and started beating his head against the sidewalk. My dad pulled the man off him and drove Fred to Doctor Redfield's. Not more than a week went by that fall without Fred rubbing the back of his head and telling me the story.

"Eighteen stitches," he'd say. "One for damn near every time I banged her."

"Was it worth it?" I finally asked him once, cutting him off before he had finished the story.

"You know what, I didn't even like her." He let out a high-pitched burst of laughter. "How about that? Had a face as ugly as homemade soap and a personality to match. I was just doing it because I could."

He rubbed his head again and began walking away. "Let that be a lesson to you: Think, don't just do."

I was only working with my dad and granddad whenever they had a prevailing-wage job. It pissed my dad off because they had a lot of work and it was football season so my brother couldn't help out, but I was flush with cash and had just got done serving my country so there wasn't much the old man could do. That didn't stop him from saying a hell of a lot, though.

Him and my granddad had been working glass so long that their hands were as tough and strong as elephant hide. About as ugly, too. They worked without gloves, picking up sheets of glass with their bare hands. And when they did, that glass would move not one inch, no matter how heavy it was or how far they had to carry it. I wasn't working enough to have gotten my hands to harden up so I had a dozen tiny slices on them all the time. At lunchtime my dad would grab me by the wrists and turn them over to inspect the cuts. He'd shake his head all disappointed like and say, "My son, the pussy." On days I knew I wouldn't be working I would stay out late the night before and stagger into the kitchen just as my dad and granddad were heading out for the day.

"Well, look who's up in time for her beauty appointment," he'd say or some other type of smart-ass remark. "Have a good day, Mary," he'd say as they left and slap me on the back of the head. Hard. Besides having hands that were all callused up, he had these thick, heavy fingers. My uncle used to tease him about them all the time. "Tell me," he'd say, "when you're playing with yourself, how do you tell the difference between your pecker and your fingers?"

It was worse with my granddad. He wouldn't even look at me, just drink his coffee and stare out at the water. He and his family barely made it through the Depression and here he was, just past seventy still working every day, so to him if you weren't helping the family bring in money or food, he had no time for you.

They were working a job in Woodland at the time. Woodland was only about thirty-five miles away as the crow flies but there was no easy way to get there from the Delta so it was over an hour drive away. If there were any hiccups on the job—and there always were—they would work fourteen hours that day and spend the night instead of driving back out there

16

on the weekend. And by spend the night I mean sleeping in the truck with the steering wheel in your gut and the gun rack in your neck. But no matter what, they'd be home for my brother's game on Friday night.

The team that year was the best we'd had in years. There was only one high school on the entire Delta and it only had four hundred and fifty students. We had to travel all over the area to play other small schools. Our favorites were when those small Christian schools would come down to play us. You know the kind—big-ass church right off the freeway with a cross four stories high, as if that meant God loved them more than you. The stands would be filled with five hundred screaming people who had been drinking since they'd gotten off work, and you'd better believe that by the time the game was over those God lovers thought they'd seen the devil himself. Around the end of the third quarter those delta breezes would be in full gear, roaring through the eucalyptus trees that lined the back of the south end zone. It was pitch dark everywhere except for the football field and when that wind would rise up out of the darkness you could tell that they thought God himself was talking to them, and not in a good way.

"Judgment day is here," we'd yell all through the fourth quarter.

My brother was five foot nine and two hundred and ten pounds, half fat, half muscle and all balls. He was big for the level we played at and started at both offensive guard and defensive tackle. He was as tough as anyone I knew. That's not to say he was a good fighter. He won more than he lost, but just barely. He could both give and take a punch but he wasn't quick and didn't have much stamina. It didn't matter because by the time he was a senior he didn't have to fight, not so much because people were afraid of him, but because they knew they would have to knock him out before he stopped coming at them. And if they did manage to take him, they'd probably have to do it at least one more time before he got the message. That was one of the things we had in common.

Anyway, my brother's team won the league championship by beating Western Christian 21-20 in the last game of the season. Western scored a touchdown with a minute left to play and went for two and the win instead of kicking the extra point for the tie and playing for overtime. After failing on the two-point conversion they tried an onside kick but my brother smothered the ball as it bounced to him and that was that. Me and my buddy Ray Thompson hid in the bushes outside the visitor's locker room and egged the bus as it headed out of town.

We felt like raising a little hell after that so we drove to South Sacramento to the Tokyo Hot Springs for a rub and tug. We both had fake IDs but everyone in town knew we were underage so we had to wait until we got to Sacramento before buying any booze. We bought a pint of Yukon Jack and poured it into our Big Gulp sodas and sat on the tailgate of the truck in the parking lot of the 7-Eleven across from the massage parlor.

Some people on the Delta never came into Sacramento; if they went anywhere it was east over to Calaveras County into the mountains. Hell, most people I knew had never been east of Reno or west of Frisco or on an airplane. Once, my cousin Tommy had a six-month roofing job in Lovelock, Nevada, and when he came home for Thanksgiving he ran into a combination of rush hour and holiday traffic in Sacramento. It scared him so much he pulled over and didn't budge until the freeways were clear. I think he got in around midnight and turned around and left after dinner the next day to avoid having to deal with any more traffic over the holiday weekend.

I liked going to Sacramento because it reminded me that I lived in the greatest place on earth. I mean, who would take concrete, traffic, heat, and living around a bunch of people who don't look like you, over the water, being able to get a gun permit from the sheriff for a case of beer, and roads with no stop lights? I watch a lot of those nature and animal channels and they go to some pretty cool places and show some pretty cool stuff, but you take it all together and there ain't no place like the Delta. Once I saw a show about this grove of aspens in

Arizona that was miles and miles long, but all the trees shared a common root so it was really one big system instead of a bunch of individual trees. It made me think of all the trees along the river. There's so many of them so close together I wouldn't be surprised if one day they find out they're like that aspen grove. One show said that even though the world is two thirds covered with water only about four percent of the people live on the water. I liked thinking I was part of such a special group.

Ray and I sat and drank and bitched about the fact that we had to drive all the way into Sacramento to get our nut. For years the Robinson house behind the laundermat had hookers. It started with the Robinson sisters, Alice and Mary, back when my granddad was full of piss and vinegar, and continued with their daughters as my daddy and my Uncle Wayne began tom-catting around back in the day. Me and Ray caught the tail end of it, even managed to sneak my brother in before the house was boarded up. The cops didn't do it—hell, Sheriff Franklin had a tab at the place. It was the women of all people who did it. The granddaughters decided if they were going to sell it, they may as well get top dollar for it, and moved to Las Vegas. I guess humping a bunch of good ol' boys with sweat on their back and whiskey on their breath wasn't their idea of living the dream. I sometimes wondered how they made out in Vegas. They all had the same big crooked nose that made them breathe loud and seem stupid, but they had this smooth dark skin and asses you could bounce a quarter off of. Some said they had Italian or Portuguese blood in them but others said it was Indian blood that gave them that skin color. Whatever it was, it was different enough from all the white okies running around the Delta to make guys keep coming back at sixty bucks a throw.

Tokyo Hot Springs had opened up while I was in the service and quickly got a reputation as a rub and tug joint. We hadn't gone yet, but with our old high school being league champions, it seemed like the right time to try it out.

Beyond the entryway, divided only by a sheet, was a hot bath big enough to fit twenty people, and six open-stall showers. We were led down a hallway that turned and split, and turned again, until reaching our rooms. I undressed down to my underwear, then folded my cash as small as I could and stuffed it into my sock and my sock into my shoe. A different woman came in after a few minutes. She pointed at my underwear and motioned for me to take them off, then handed me a robe. I followed her down the hallway and soon we were back at the bath. Ray was already in it, drinking a beer.

"Another one for league champions," he said, raising his beer to one of the women lingering around the tub. I had already lost count of how many I'd seen. They were all small, Asian, and quiet with skin that had shied away from the sun at every opportunity. They seemed to be in every shadow, every corner of the place. Guys in the service told me about these huge whorehouses in the Philippines, a couple of acres of pussy and rotgut booze under a tin roof. For twenty-five dollars, they said, you could have as many throws as you could manage in a twenty-four hour period. The only thing that got in the way, they claimed, was the rain hitting the tin roof like a million pellets all at once. There was no way, they said, a guy could keep his rhythm when the rain really came down. I never got out of the States during my two years so I had to settle for the strip joints and massage parlors that were on the edge of every military base I've ever seen.

After we finished our beers we were taken to the showers, lathered up then dried off and led back to our rooms. After about ten minutes of massaging, the woman nudged me to roll over on my back and said the only words spoken to me the entire night. "You want me to massage that, too?"

I nodded and she took me in her hands for a few moments then stopped. "You give me tip?"

Now that's a pro, I thought. I would've signed over my truck right about then. "Of course," I said in a high-pitched voice and she picked up where she had left off.

We headed back home on Highway 12. It always made me laugh, the way the name of the highway changed right after the city limits of Sacramento. The road was the same, only smaller without streetlights on it or any shoulder to speak of. The city didn't even bother giving it a name; everyone just called it the river road. Many a night my dad had gotten a call to grab his winch and pull a buddy out of the bank before he slid into the river. And of course, there were many a night we had to call those same friends to get my daddy or granddad or uncle. If it wasn't the dark and the curves that got you, the tule fog or the drinking surely would.

Ray hit the steering wheel with his palm and started chuckling. "I tell you, as long as I live I'll never forget seeing you in the shower, that little gal stroking your johnson. It was as hard as all get out and you had the biggest shit-eating grin on your face."

"I've got two questions for you," I said. "One, what the hell were you doing looking at me when you had your own gal lathering you up, and why didn't you have a hard-on?"

"Because this wasn't my first rodeo. I don't get all excited the first time a gal touches me."

"Well, then, I feel sorry for you buddy."

"No need. I get my money's worth out of places like this. Speaking of that, how much did you pay?" Ray asked.

"Twenty."

"Hah! Rookie. For thirty I got her to go down on me."

"No shit? Hell, I had forty on me."

"Did you even ask?"

I shook my head and knew I was in for a night of sarcastic comments about my lack of brains.

"Should we try to sneak into Fred's or go to the Buckhorn?" Ray asked. "I'm not too drunk. I can make the drive."

Before I could answer, we came around a corner by old man Stephen's place and saw my brother sitting on the side of the road.

"What the hell are you doing, pulling your pud?" Ray said. My brother was on my side of the truck and I could tell something was wrong.

He was hunched over in a ball, holding himself tight, almost rocking. "What's going on, Brother?" I asked, my voice flat. I wasn't trying to sound calm—I was calm.

A guy I went through basic training with died after a day of hiking with a full backpack in over one hundred-degree weather. We were back at the barracks, still red and sweating even though we'd just gotten out of the shower.

"Look at Jimmy, sleeping over there like a baby," someone said. "Wake him up so we can play cards. We need a pigeon."

I snapped him hard with my towel. Too hard. A red welt appeared instantly on his shoulder. I hoped he wouldn't want to fight over it, not because I didn't think I could take him, but because I liked him and had no energy in me after the hike. He didn't move and someone shook him by the shoulders and rolled him over. He was foaming from the mouth. The guy jumped back like a snake had bit him.

"Holy shit! Something's wrong. Holy shit."

"What do we do? Someone give him mouth to mouth."

"Fuck you. You give it to him."

"Go get the duty officer," I said. "Let's roll him on his stomach so he doesn't choke."

I didn't have any first aid training and it wasn't like I grew up seeing people die every day, but something inside me knew that this wasn't the worst of it. For him maybe, lying on his bed, probably already dead, but the hard part for the rest of us was still ahead. Things like death and divorce and fights that ended friendships, or getting fired, those things were the beginning, not the end of the shit storm so there wasn't much use in getting too crazy about them while they were happening.

Jimmy Patterson was eighteen and from some wide spot in the road in Kansas. He could play the hell out of the harmonica and guitar, and was a pretty fair singer, I thought. But his daddy thought all musicians were hippies who wore earrings in the wrong ear, so the day after graduating from high school young Jimmy was marched down to the local Army recruiting office and signed up. Who knows if he would've become a famous musician, or just another guy who played with his buddies on the weekends, or something in between, but as he lay dead in front of me I thought he's either hanging out with God

22

now or things have just gone dark in his brain, but either way it was over for him. But when the Army called his mom and dad later that day, they would have questions for themselves and each other that would never get answered. That's what his parents had to look forward to.

I was thinking about all that as I got out of the truck and walked to my brother. "I thought you'd be out with the team celebrating."

He pointed to the river. He was soaking wet, water running off his shaking index finger. I followed his finger down the bank and saw mud gouged with tire marks and tree branches torn away. But no car. I ran down to the river, slipping and tearing open my forearm on a branch. I didn't see a car or air bubbles or anything. Ray met me as I was making my way back up to the road.

"What's going on?" he asked. "I can't get a word out of your brother."

"They're in the river," I said.

"Who?"

"I don't know, but they ain't coming up."

We called the sheriff, then Ray moved his truck as close to the bank as he dared and pointed the headlights toward the water. The low beams didn't have enough juice to reach the water, the light losing itself in the mud of the bank before hitting the river, and the high beams floated out above the water, leaving only our fear to visualize what had happened down below. We broke off the biggest branch we could and Ray waded into the river as far as he was able and started poking and thrashing about with it in hopes of hitting something we could dive for. After a few minutes I left Ray to see about my brother. He sat looking straight at the river and all I could get out of him were one-word whispers.

"Who were you with?"

"Johnny."

"Who was driving?"

"Me."

"What happened?"

"Tire."

Sheriff Franklin arrived first, followed closely by the volunteer fire department and Haley's Tow Service. With the proper lighting, it didn't take long to find the truck. As the tow truck pulled my daddy's truck from the river with Johnny inside it, the sheriff turned his attention to my brother.

"After we get you stitched up we'll need to take a blood sample."

It was then I noticed the gash on my brother's head. It was the size of a small rock and about as deep. Years later, my parents would blame the doctors or the medication for what became of my brother, but standing on that river bank that night, I knew he was already gone. His eyes were dead and all the fight in him had been drowned in the river with Johnny. I never told my parents any of that, not that night or any other night.

"What the hell for?" I said to Franklin.

"You know what the hell for."

"He said it was a blowout. You can see the tire from here. Look at the skid marks on the road, for Christ's sake."

Franklin didn't answer, which put my anger into high gear. I stepped close to him, closer than a smart man should step to a cop, but my brother was already gone, I didn't see the need to actually bury him that night.

"Why don't you let him be, Franklin? The worst has already been done to him."

"Because that's not the way it works. You have to answer for everything." He looked at the truck then at my brother. "Look, these are your options. You can continue to stand this close to me and go to the station with your brother and take the same tests I'm going to give him, or you can go home and tell your momma and daddy what has happened."

I may be dumb but I'm not stupid. I walked away from Franklin to the truck.

Turned out my brother hadn't been speeding or was drunk. The blood alcohol sample came back at .07, just under the legal limit, so all was good on that front. The blowout was on the passenger side, and my brother over-compensated when he felt the truck pull to the right. The truck cut across the road and pitched over the side down the bank. The vehicle rolled, tossing my brother out of the driver's side window before hitting the water. My brother was knocked out for a moment because he said the next thing he remembered after the blowout was seeing the tailgate of the truck sink below the surface of the water. He wasn't the best swimmer anyway, and in the dark he never even got to the truck.

We spent the next week alone in our house. I think it was the only time we ever spent that much time alone together in that house. I couldn't remember it happening any time before, and I sure as hell know it hasn't happened since. The only television was in the living room, which opened into the dining room and kitchen. My brother spent most of the time in his room, though I'm not certain he was sleeping. When he did come out we sat in a circle around the television, not taking our eyes off it even during commercials. Occasionally me or my mom or dad would get up to go to the bathroom or get something from the kitchen. Our movements were deliberate and silent so as not to startle my brother or make him think of moving back to his room. After dinner my parents would sit at the dining room table and smoke and have a cup of coffee. I could sense them looking at my brother but I was in their sightline too, and it made me sit even more still than I had been. My brother didn't seem to notice or care. The dining room was too close to the living room for them to talk without us hearing, so they just sat, drinking and smoking and staring.

The phone rang a lot that week. My dad was pressuring the insurance company for a check so he could buy a truck and get back to work, but most of the calls were my brother's friends checking up on him. The only words out of my mom's mouth were, "He's fine," or "He's sleeping." A few friends of the family stopped by, always unannounced, as was the custom in town. The knock on the door was always startling, like an act of aggression. My mom would open the door and step outside, closing it behind her, never allowing anyone inside.

Our house was never quiet like that, and it made me jumpy; I could just imagine what it was doing to my brother. But I never got a chance to talk to him. The one time I started to make my way to his room, my mom stopped me dead with a sharp clearing of her throat and a stare I'd never seen out of her. Her face was tight, her eyes dull and empty, almost lifeless, like she had already played it out in her mind how poorly everything would end for my brother but was still determined to see it through with him. I never tried to talk to him alone after that, even if I thought my mom was wrong. Me and him never had a whole lot of deep conversations, but I felt I knew him as well as anybody—and believed I could've helped him, even if it was just by listening. But I was only twenty and she was my mom, so I did what she wanted. Whenever my brother did come out to watch television with us, to try to talk to him in front of my parents would have been to tackle the whole thing all at once, something that was much too big for all of us right then. Hell, it might have always been too big for us, but I've always thought we should've at least given it a try.

After four nights hunkered down in the house, something had to give. My parents' fights were always over little, bullshit things, but they argued loudly and neither would give in so the fights usually lasted multiple days. But for four days they had been excessively polite to each other, which only added to the tension. So on the fourth night me and my dad started drinking beer early in the afternoon and instinctively graduated to whiskey after dinner.

"Go outside if you're determined to get piss drunk tonight," my mom said as she cleaned off the kitchen table. Normally that would get my dad barking back about her not telling him what to do in his own house, being a grown man and all, but instead he went out the slider without a word, leaving it open for me to follow. We sat on the deck overlooking the river thirty feet below us, a bucket of ice, some soda, and a bottle of

Jack Daniels between us. The sun soon disappeared behind the trees, and unlike during the summer when that signaled the rise of the wind off the water, come fall and winter those same breezes were swallowed by the river, leaving nights the same temperature as the day.

After about an hour of drinking—never fully finishing our drinks, but topping them off when they were nearly gone—my dad went to the edge of the deck and pissed in the river. He put his hand on my shoulder as he sat back down, and I wasn't sure if he meant to or just needed help getting back into his chair.

"Your brother will get through this," he said.

I nodded. I almost said I hope so, but didn't want to sound negative.

"It sounds cold-hearted, but the best thing for him would be to forget it ever happened."

"How the hell's he supposed to do that?" I said. It was a cold-hearted thing for him to say, and my objection was out of my mouth before I could take a drink and drown it.

"Listen, boy," my dad said, stabbing his finger at me but looking at the river, "nothing is ever built on looking backwards. Not a business, not a family, nothing. You can't live life looking over your shoulder."

We topped off our drinks and went back to staring at the river.

Finally, my dad said, "He just needs to get through this year, get in the Army and get away from here for a while. Maybe even do two hitches, be gone four, five, six years."

When I didn't respond, he continued talking.

"See," he said, "your brother is good at doing what he's told. A helluva lot better at it than you, I can tell you that. It'll all be about what everyone at school and in town thinks. If they think it's his fault, he'll start thinking the same way."

"What do you think?"

"Goddamn it, didn't you just hear what I said? It doesn't matter what the fuck I think or what you or your mom think. All that matters is what he thinks."

There were two memorial services for Johnny that week, one at the high school and one at the cemetery. No one from our family went to either one. My brother was in no shape, and though my parents disagreed as to why we shouldn't go, they both agreed we should stay home. My dad thought our presence might be seen as an act of guilt while my mom was afraid we wouldn't be welcome.

"I tell you what, just let one of those in-bred, scissor jacks look cross-eyed at me, and we'll have us a problem," my dad said.

"Don't go getting yourself all worked up before anything has happened," my mom said.

"Well, I'm just letting you know where I stand."

"I swear, you men in this family. You talk yourself into a fight, then if it doesn't show up, you go find one."

"Hell, woman, why are you bringing up shit like that now?"

"It's shit like that that makes it tough to stick together is all I'm trying to say."

And off they went, arguing about things that had nothing to do with the accident, or things that had taken place years ago, until the house was filled with curses and accusations, and then a long, long silence.

The only time someone left the house was at the end of the week when the insurance money came. My dad called my Uncle Wayne and they didn't return home until dark, pulling up in a brand new Dodge Ram. My dad teetered up the walkway while my uncle set off down the road. My dad's eyes turned red and glassy when the porch light hit, the veins little red rivulets extending from the center of them.

My mom met him at the door. "Go all the way to Detroit to get that, did you?"

"Just about. South Sac," my dad said. He kissed her cheek as he moved past her into the house.

"Where's my brother going?"

"On a little walk about. You know how he gets."

"You know," my mom said, "drinking vodka to hide the smell only works if you can walk straight." But my dad was

28

already down the hall towards their bedroom. He stopped at my brother's door, peeked in quickly, then continued on.

My mom went back to washing the dinner dishes, scrubbing the plates harder than needed, muttering, "Man can't even manage to stay with his family for seven whole days. Like it's some kind of goddamn prison sentence."

I turned the television up a click so she could rant in private. I wondered why my dad hadn't taken me along with him—he knew I was going just as stir-crazy as he was—when I remembered that the Dodge dealership in South Sacramento was a block away from the Tokyo Hot Springs. I wasn't mad at him. A man who makes his own money deserves the right to spend it any way he wants. But I hoped when I was his age I was still not like a dog chasing my own tail. I thought all the hell-raising a man did in his younger days was meant to get it out of his system so he could move on to the next thing, not make it a permanent part of him.

Monday morning, ten days after the accident, my dad woke at five o'clock and put on his work clothes. He had a strip mall to get to after the job in Woodland, then jobs in Davis and Sacramento waiting behind that one, so it was all hands on deck for the next six months. Even my Uncle Wayne would be working full time.

My mom had got up with him to make a pot of coffee, and I came out of my room to see what was going on. "We've got plenty of work if you can find time out of your busy schedule, Nancy," he said.

"I was thinking I'd stick close to home for a little while longer," I said.

"Don't make a thing of it, all right? With you and your mom hovering around him all the time, he'll start thinking it was his fault. I always liked Johnny, even if his dad is a bit on the queer side. I'm sorry he's gone, I really am. But it was an accident. Leave it at that."

My dad stood in the kitchen and stared at me like he was the rightest man in the world. I turned and went back to my room and got dressed for work.

It wasn't too long before the crying started. We'd be woken in the middle of the night by it and find my brother sitting on the couch in his underwear, bawling like a newborn baby. We couldn't get him to talk, so we'd just sit at the kitchen table and watch him. Sometimes my dad would put on a pot of coffee then signal it was time for us to go to work. Other times he'd get up out of his chair after about twenty or thirty minutes of it, pat my mom's shoulder, and head off to bed. My mom never left until my brother stopped crying. I'd hear them shuffle off to his room, her arm around him, I imagined, and I would hear her tuck him in, though I could never quite make out what she said to him.

One night, through all the tears and snot running down his nose, my brother said, "The front windshield was nearly kicked out."

When we didn't respond, he continued. "The cops told me Johnny tried to kick the front windshield out to escape. They said there were fingernail scratch marks all over the dashboard."

My mom went to the couch and hugged my brother harder than any hit he'd ever taken on the football field. My father came over and shooed her away. "Son," he said, "it's time to clean it up."

He stood and pointed a finger at my brother, who wasn't crying anymore, but whimpering with his head tucked into his chest. "Listen, I'm sorry for what happened. I'm sorry you've had to go through this. It's a shitty situation all around. But after tonight I don't want any more crying."

My brother made it through the school year, though I could still hear him crying at night in his room, muffling the sound with his pillow. I went in and sat with him a few times but he never said a word about the accident or anything else.

He went into the Army after graduation, but was sent home soon after boot camp with a letter saying he was unfit for duty. I gotta give my dad credit, he never gave him any shit for washing out, but you could tell by the way he looked at him when he thought no one was watching that he thought my brother was damaged goods.

He came to work with us, and at times it was like the accident had never happened. We worked hard, made decent money, and he was even losing some of his baby fat. My brother was always a little on the quiet side compared to me and my dad, but we'd have a couple of beers on the ride home and he'd wait for the right moment and jump in with one of his sarcastic remarks. Then, out of the blue, he'd wake up one morning and refuse to go to work. He'd lie in bed without an expression on his face as my dad yelled and cursed at him. But he was like a mule that had decided enough was enough. Eventually, one of those days stretched into two weeks. My parents took him to see a doctor in Sacramento who kept him in the psych ward for observation.

A week later we were coming home from a job in Lincoln, driving on Highway 80 through Sacramento. "Think we should stop by the hospital?" I said.

My dad kept driving, his eyes never leaving the road. "Your brother is in Napa at the state mental hospital."

"When did this happen?"

"Day before yesterday. Doctors say he needs full-time help."

"When were you going to tell me?"

"I'm telling you now."

I was mad like right before the first punch was thrown in a fight, but it was my dad so I ate my anger. I turned and looked out the window and we didn't speak until on the job the next day.

I got an offer to work on the new casino that was being built in Reno. It seemed like a good time to get out of town—Ray was holed up with his new girlfriend, and now that I was twenty-one, Fred's wasn't nearly as exciting as before. Taking the job in Reno meant I'd have to join the union. I figured my dad was going to give me hell for leaving him short-handed and joining a union, but when I told him about the job he just nodded and patted me on the shoulder, like he wished he could leave with me.

I saw my brother at Christmas, before I left town. He was sluggish in a way that had nothing to do with the thirty pounds he had gained. They had him on all kinds of medication that didn't seem to be helping.

"How's it going, Chief?" I said, slapping his knee. "Please tell me you're banging some of these nurses."

We were outside. Even though it was winter the Napa Valley was still mostly green, the hills surrounding the valley calm and full of promise, waiting patiently for spring to introduce itself. It was about sixty degrees, and if I weren't at a mental hospital visiting my brother, I'd say it was just about the most beautiful place I'd ever seen.

My brother looked at me, gave a hint of a smile and a chuckle but neither quite happened.

"What do you say, think you'll be home for Easter?"

He didn't speak for a long time. I was about to repeat my question when he said, "I never liked Easter much. "

"Yeah?"

"Too hard to find those eggs with my color blindness," he said, his words coming out slowly.

"But mom's honey-glazed ham tastes better than most of the pussy I've had."

"I like turkey better," he said.

He began rocking back and forth. His eyes were glassy. There was nothing registering in his head or heart that resembled the brother I knew. I sat for a while looking at the rolling hills around us then back to my brother before getting up and leaving. I didn't even say goodbye.

I never knew the exact diagnosis they gave my brother but it didn't take a doctor to see he wasn't getting better. He had no desire to get out or get better, or even any clue what "better" meant. I said earlier that even though my brother was tough, he wasn't much of a fighter. He'd get his ass kicked and show up to school or work the next day as if nothing had happened. When I lost a fight I couldn't wait to have another one to wipe the taste out of my mouth. Luckily, I'd never lost two fights in

32

a row. I don't know what I'd do if I did, just keep looking for trouble until I found some I could handle, no matter what punishment I had to take. I had always admired my brother's ability to not take personal getting his ass kicked, but when I saw him in Napa I wished he had a little more fight in him.

"How was he?" my mom asked when I got home.

"Okay," I said. "He can't wait to be home at Easter for your ham."

In the spring I got a call from my dad telling me my brother had hanged himself in his room. "When you get here," he told me, "tell your mother you love her but don't talk about your brother. She's about ready to break wide open."

When I arrived she hugged me tight around the neck and half whispered, half sobbed in my ear, "He never liked my ham, you know. He always liked turkey better."

Turned out I was the one who cracked. The next few months were lost to drinking and getting arrested, in that order. Strangely, there were no fights. I either drank in my apartment alone or at one of the dives in downtown Reno, the kind of places people stay hunched over their drink for hours and hours and no one talks much to anyone. At those places, patrons weren't on their way to someplace; the bar was there and so were they. My granddad died of a heart attack during that time but I barely remember it, even now. All I can really remember is how much I wanted to sleep. If I wasn't drunk I had no chance of sleeping. I would spend hours staring at the clock, trying to think of anything except my brother. When I was able to nod off, the sleep was a fitful spurt of dreams about him.

I began drinking in order to sleep without dreaming, but almost every time I opened a bottle I ended up taking too much of it. I would wake on the floor or the couch and feel as if I hadn't slept at all. I didn't talk to my parents much during all that time. My dad was really short-handed once my grandfather passed, plus he liked being out—be it working, fishing, or holding court at Fred's. He viewed home as a place to eat breakfast and dinner—and to sleep before doing it all over again the next day. Whenever I talked to my mom, she would go on and on about every little thing in her day or what was going on around town. She talked quickly, never letting much space develop between subjects. Once she had exhausted herself, there would be a giant pause before one of us would say, okay, then. I guess I'll talk to you later, and we'd hang up.

I got popped three times for drinking and driving before my license was yanked. Looking back on it, Reno was probably the worst place to be while trying to deal with my brother's death. It's billed as the "Biggest Little City in the World," and that's the way it felt. Plenty of bars and casinos to get into trouble for sure, but the city was surrounded by the flat high desert, which made it feel small in comparison to its surroundings. Closed in, when all I wanted was to be free. I swear, I could stand in the bed of my truck and see the entire city. Every part of it seemed accessible and too many times I got in my car after drinking to see what was happening in the part of town I wasn't in. I would hit the casinos after work, holes in my jeans and dirt in every line in my skin, and drink as many free drinks as I could before losing forty dollars at the blackjack table. Then I'd get serious about getting drunk.

Getting so many DUIs in such a short time kicked them up to a felony. I was given six months in county jail plus a year's probation and I had to take all kinds of classes to get my license back. I had never been to jail. The closest I'd ever gotten was six hours in juvenile detention in West Sacramento. Me and Ray were seniors in high school and were trying out our fake IDs when we got pulled over. Ray was driving and had just turned eighteen so off to jail he went. I was two weeks away from my birthday—don't tell me luck doesn't play into things—and was sent to juvi instead. I almost didn't call my parents. I figured the old man would let me stay in the "county hotel," as he called jail, for the weekend to teach me a lesson, but I didn't want my mom to worry about me not coming home all night. But damn if he didn't show up less than an hour after

I called. Of course he slapped me upside the head as we walked to the truck and worked my ass off around the house the next day. I had to wash his truck, clean the gutters, and scrub the floor of the garage. That was okay. I still got off easier than Ray. He blew a .16 blood alcohol content and was sentenced to six weekends of picking up trash alongside Highway 80, attend a bunch of AA meetings, and had to pay a five-hundred-dollar fine.

Just because I'd never spent a night in jail didn't meant I hadn't deserved to. But on the Delta, Sheriff Franklin still let you pour out your beer while he threatened to call your parents, and in the Army it was almost expected of you to raise a little hell. A fight or a summons for pissing in the alley outside a bar was met with a shake of the head and a smile by your sergeant.

I was nervous when I showed up that first day, but it wasn't bad. I mean other than having no freedom for one hundred and eighty days. You hear those stories of guys who had spent so much time locked up that they couldn't hack it on the outside. That blows my mind, how someone could get used to having no freedom, to having every minute of the day laid out by someone else. But people get married and work jobs they hate for their whole lives, so what the hell do I know?

I was in jail, not prison, so there weren't too many tough guys around. Between the god-awful food and not being able to drink, I lost fifteen pounds. And after a couple of weeks, I was able to piece together three or four hours of sleep in a row for the first time since my brother had killed himself.

The union still had plenty of work in Reno and said I had a job waiting for me when I got out. My mom wanted me home but for the first time in my life I didn't feel like being on the Delta. It was the end of winter and everything would be wet and dirty and smothered by the tule fog. I couldn't stand the thought of hanging out at Fred's and hearing people talk about my brother. Or worse, not talk about him. After getting out of jail I took the bus back and forth to work and cabs downtown on the weekends, figuring I'd flip the script on my luck. It almost worked.

I caught the bus at the Peppermill every day after work. I'd go inside and play the same progressive slot machine while waiting for my ride. One day, about six months after I had gotten out, this guy was playing my machine. I got a drink and played the machine next to him. I had taken up drinking again, but not like before, and at least I wasn't driving. After more than three I couldn't stop thinking about my brother, and I was getting tired of feeling sad all the time. Then I'd feel guilty about not wanting to be sad, like I was leaving my brother behind. Then I'd get mad at myself, which I could never hold inside very long without putting it out into the world. I hadn't gotten in a fight since I'd been out, but the walls of my apartment had taken more than a few punches.

The guy on my machine hit a jackpot for ten thousand dollars. I couldn't fucking believe it! It was like the world was laughing at me while flipping me off. Ten thousand dollars! After all the money I'd spent on my arrests. I thought of my brother and how he mindlessly took all those pills the doctors shoved down his throat and the next thing I knew I was slamming that guy's head against the slot machine that had given him my money.

I spent six weekends in jail for assault plus had my probation extended a year. After that little stint in jail I took to going home every other weekend. I had been up in Reno almost two years at that point and had almost forgotten how much better the summers were on the Delta. Winters in Reno were great: sun almost every day with snow on the mountains all around you. Most of my work was partially indoors, and I worked every minute of eight hours a day, so the cold never bothered me. But come summertime, when the hot wind blew through town during the day and nothing blew through at night, there was no way of getting around the fact that you were in the desert. High desert or not, it was still the desert in the summer.

When I came home I'd usually spend Friday night at Fred's, whooping it up with Ray and other old buddies. We still weren't talking about my brother. I think Ray was waiting for me to bring it up, but I figured everyone is going to have some rough patches in their lives, why should my family and I be any different? And how would crying in my beer make anything any better? Saturday nights I spent at my parents' house. After dinner I'd sit on the back deck and watch the river slide by and let the delta breezes do their magic. Sometimes my mom or dad—but never both—would come out and sit with me. We'd sit well past dark without speaking or moving, as if we both wanted the peace of the river to ourselves and were trying to outlast the other.

Towards the end of fall, as I was getting ready to catch the bus back up the hill to Reno, my mother said to me, "Your father sure could use you down here."

"That union money is hard to pass up," I said. "Besides, he's got Uncle Wayne to help him, right?"

"You know how they fight when they spend too much time around each other."

"Another year, Ma, maybe two, and I can come back with enough money that we can get another truck, expand the business."

She had her back to me, putting together a bag of food for the trip and when she turned around she was smiling, but it was a sad smile. When she used to talk my brother out of his crying fits she would get close to his face and say as many encouraging things as she could get out in one breath. She would be smiling all the time but it was a scared smile, as if she knew her time to save him was short.

"We all miss you around here," she said.

My dad honked the car to tell me it was time to get to the station. I hugged her and said, "I love you, Ma."

She held onto me tight while my dad honked again. "Be good," she whispered in my ear.

Snow came the next weekend, and the Donner Pass became its annual mess so I stayed in Reno until Christmas. My last night home over the Christmas holiday was spent hanging out with Ray. After cruising up and down the river road looking for anything exciting, we ended up at Fred's. As we walked in, the first person I saw was Hank Unger. I should've turned around and walked out right then, but I didn't want him thinking I was running from him.

We had first tangled when I was a freshman in high school and he stole some beer from me and some friends at a party. He was already out of school but I went for him anyway. He was much taller than me and held me at arm's length as I cursed and swung wildly at him, hitting nothing but air. My senior year I ran into him at a party after a football game and made amends. By then I was too strong for him to hold off. I got him to the ground and gave him a pretty good beating. He tried me again right after I got back from the service. He was about six foot two with sharp boney hands, and if I could get into him quick, I was okay, but if he got the first shot in and stayed away from me, I would be in trouble. He got in a couple of weak-ass jabs on me as I lowered my head and drove into him, but the fight got broken up before I could do any damage to him.

"Maybe you ought to quit fighting tall guys," my dad said the next day when he saw my swollen lip.

"Or better yet, stop fighting all together," my mom said.

Being only five foot eight, not fighting tall guys wasn't much of an option, and being a pussy and not standing my ground was even less of one. My strategy was simple: Once the action started, I would take as many punches as I had to in order to get inside. Everyone in town knew this about me—which was why I hadn't fought anyone from town, other than Hank Unger, in years.

"Your boy is here," Ray said as we ordered beers and shots at the bar.

"Just my luck," I said. "Don't even look at him. I got no need for him tonight. Tell me something new that's going on around town."

"Let's see. Oh, the sheriff has his panties in bunch because the *Sacramento Bee* did a big article on how easy it is to get a concealed-weapon permit down here."

"What business is it of theirs? It's not like people have shoot-outs in the streets."

Ray shrugged. "The article said something like seventy percent of males over eighteen have a permit down here, compared to five percent in the rest of the state. So now he's looking for any excuse to revoke a permit."

"Well, they already got mine."

"How so?"

"That third drunk-driving made me a felon," I said and threw back my shot. "I can no longer carry a gun or run for president."

"Too bad," Ray laughed. "You would've had my vote."

It wasn't but a few minutes later that I received a hard slap on the back. "Well, if it ain't my old pal," Hank said.

"I'm sorry," I said, "do we know each other?"

"Hank Unger," he said, taking a half step back to make sure I could see all of him.

"Did we go to school together? Are you a glazier?"

"The party out at the swimming hole? You telling me you don't remember that?"

"Sorry, friend. I've been gone a few years. There's a lot about this place I don't know about anymore."

He smiled—smirked, really—and shook his head. "Okay. Okay. If that's what you're about now, then fine."

I had him; I had him good. But that goddamn smirk. If it were anyone else I could let the guy walk away and think whatever he thought.

"Frank," I said.

He turned around. "Hank."

"That's what I meant."

"I'm sure you did."

"I was wondering if I could buy you a beer."

"Sure," he said, his eyes going every which way trying to figure out what I was up to.

"Or do you still prefer to steal your beer?" I said and threw my beer in his face. I charged him, plowing my head into his chest and driving him the length of the bar until I rammed his back against the knob on the bathroom door.

He grunted, and I flew my head straight up into his chin and heard his teeth crack against each other. He tried to break free, pounding on my back, but I had a hold of his neck and down to the floor we went. I bounced his head off the floor three or four times before the bartender and a couple of other guys pulled me off.

I was pushed into one corner and Hank into another. He had no blood on him but his face was red and his eyes a little glassy.

"You cold-cocking little bitch. Too afraid to come at me straight."

I charged him, got a few feet before those holding me back stopped me. "I'll fight you anytime, anywhere you cock-sucker," I yelled. "You know who I am! You know who I am!" I was blind mad. Crazy mad. Stupid mad. Too mad for my own good, or anyone else's. There was no calming down, there was only getting it out of my system. "I'll fucking kill you. You know I'll kill you!" I screamed.

"Stay on both of them till the sheriff gets here," Fred said.

"What the fuck, Fred," Ray said. "It's a goddamn fight on a Saturday night."

"Sheriff says he wants to know everything that happens from now on."

Franklin arrived in a few minutes. I had stopped screaming at Unger but wasn't any less pissed. "Bring 'em outside, boys," he said and we were taken out back, facing the river.

"Anyone here sober enough to drive home?" Franklin asked.

The men who had a hold of me loosened their grip and I charged Unger and kicked him straight in the balls. He crumbled and before I could get another shot in on him the sheriff slapped me across the face. It startled me more than if he had pepper sprayed me or knocked me across the knees with his nightstick. I stood in front of him, shocked and suddenly sober.

"Get the fuck back there," he said as the men grabbed me and dragged me back to where I had been. He turned to Hank, then back to me, "What the hell are you thinking?"

"That's the second time that mother fucker…" Hank said.

"I don't give a rat's ass about a stupid bar fight," Franklin said. "Either of you got anything illegal on you or in your car?"

"How 'bout you, Unger? You're a pothead, if I remember right," Franklin said, lifting him up till he was standing. He patted Hank's pockets and found a baggie of pot in the front pocket of his flannel shirt.

"Jesus, there ain't enough in there to make a decent joint," Hank said.

"But plenty to give me probable cause to search your car," the sheriff said. "Keys."

There was no dope in Unger's car but he did have a pearl-handle .22 pistol under the driver's seat.

"You got a permit for this?" Franklin asked.

"You gave me one for my twenty-first birthday," Unger said.

"Looks like you boys are going downtown," Franklin said.

They put me in Franklin's car. "Why do I have to go in?" I asked as we pulled away from Fred's. "Like you said, it was just a bar fight."

"I'm taking Hank's permit, and to do that I have to search his car. The pot he had on him gives me cause to search his car, the fight gives me cause to search him."

"I'm on probation, you know."

He nodded.

"Can't you leave me out of it, somehow?"

"I'd look pretty stupid filing a report about a guy fighting himself."

"You're really fucking me, you know that."

He shook his head. "Nope."

"What do you mean, nope?"

"Oh, you're fucked alright, son, but I'm not the one doing it."

And that was how I got my probation extended another year.

I couldn't stand the thought of another winter in Reno so I moved home in the fall. I was flush with cash so I bought a new truck and some equipment and fixed up our garage so it was a real nice work area. Things were slow to pick up that first winter back so my dad recommended I put my name in at the union hall in Sacramento, which shocked the hell out of me.

"No use both of us being broke," he said.

I didn't do it. I figured it took a lot for him to say that to me, so out of respect for him, I didn't do it. Instead we hunkered down like we'd done a handful of times, like almost everyone on the Delta had done at some point in their life. We ate a lot of spaghetti and soup and leftovers of both. We watched television instead of going to the movies, didn't buy any new clothes, drank at home instead of going to Fred's and cut down on our smoking. If we were really hard up we'd buy generic cigarettes.

We may have been used to doing without, but that didn't mean we enjoyed it. Every couple of weeks we'd find ourselves at Fred's, blowing off steam with what little money we had. One Friday night I walked into Fred's and walked out with Kathy McPherson. She was two years ahead of me in school and had dark red hair that hung straight and flat down her back and past her hips.

I didn't even talk to her until the end of the night, though I noticed her right away when she walked in. It was impossible not to, she and her two friends were the best looking split tail to have graced the bar in some time. Plus, they stayed all night, which was a rarity for most women in town. Seemed the

42

tougher times got down here, the more the men wanted to be together even if it meant a fight would eventually break out, while the women wanted to be alone. It was as if the woman were waiting out the storm while we needed to believe we were doing something, anything, even if it didn't help one bit.

Anyway, I was hanging with Ray and a few old timers, playing darts, shaking dice for drinks, talking too loud, trying to be funny, when I made my way to the jukebox. Kathy had gotten there just before me and turned to me as I approached.

"Finally going to talk to me, huh?" she said.

"I was taught never to look upper classmen in the eye," I said.

"Is that why you've been staring at my tits all night?"

"What? I didn't even know you were in the bar till just now!"

She laughed. "I know. I'm just busting your chops."

"But you have been staring at me," she said.

"You're one to talk," I said. "I've felt your eyes on my ass all night."

She laughed again and I felt my chest fill. "We'll agree to disagree."

The clock above the jukebox said 1:30. "We only have time for one song," she said. "You pick."

"What are you talking about, sweetheart? Fred's goes all the way till 2:00."

"Really? I'll have to come back more often."

"Why would anyone leave in the first place?" I said.

"You'd never know what you were missing if you never left."

"A smart person would."

"You were in Reno for a few years, weren't you?"

"I said a smart man, not me."

She punched a button on the jukebox and Bob Seger's "Old Time Rock and Roll" started playing. "Are you smart enough to dance with me?" she asked, and off we went.

We spent the rest of the weekend together, lying in bed during the day and driving up and down the river at night. We rolled down the windows to let the air pass through the cab of my truck. It was cold enough so that your cheeks felt like they had been slapped a time or two but not so much that you didn't want to be awake and close to the river to enjoy it. Outside was a wall of black, but we always knew where we were on the river as we drove it from Sacramento to Martinez and back. It was just as dark inside the truck, which allowed me to stare at Kathy as she talked.

We came around a sharp turn a dozen miles south of town, and I pointed to a squatty eucalyptus tree across the road. "Benson," I said.

"I saw him earlier that night. He was already drunker than a thousand Indians," Kathy said.

"Crazy the way that tree has never grown right since," I said.

"Yeah, it's not like it's the first tree run into on this road."

The few times I'd actually dated a girl, it came about when I didn't try too hard. Trying too hard usually ended up with me drinking too much and saying something stupid, or trying for something more than a kiss when I probably could've gotten everything I wanted on the next date if I had just settled for that kiss on the first date. Then, no one would ever accuse me of looking at the long term in any walk of my life. As far as I could figure, Kathy must have liked my look and heard me bullshitting with the boys and thought I was interesting. I had decided not to think too much about what might be happening between us and just go with it, to not pre-plan anything to say, but to pretend I had nothing to prove to her, that I was already whole without her.

"That was the first and only time I ever saw my dad cry," I said. "He came home that night and sat on the edge of his bed and sobbed like a baby. My mom rubbed his back but he couldn't stop. Him and Kent's dad had been tight all the way back to kindergarten. He quit the fire department after that."

"What about when your brother died?"

I reached across the back of the cab and put my hand deep into her hair. I was already wondering what it would feel like to

44

get lost in her hair, have it tumble down on me from above, walk my fingers through it in search of her, not minding if I stayed lost.

"I don't know," I said. "I was up in Reno when it happened." A few beats passed. My uncle had once told me that the ideal woman is one who would know enough to be quiet when you told her to be quiet. Right then I wanted Kathy to keep asking me questions.

Finally, I said, "I know I sure did. It took me most of a year to be able to say his name out loud."

"I'm sorry," she said. "It was a terrible thing. All of it."

"Let me ask you something." I took a deep breath. "Do people in town blame my brother?"

She shook her head. "I can't speak for the Murphy family, but no."

"He had been drinking," I said. "He wasn't drunk, but he had been drinking." I felt as if I was betraying my brother by even bringing it up.

"This fucking town," she said. The velocity of her words caused me to withdraw my hand from her hair. "I can't remember any of my cousins getting past the age of twelve without having a beer put in their hands by an uncle or friend of the family. 'Here, boy, it'll put hair on your chest.' Ho, ho, ho. I truly believe my brother had no choice but to be a drunk. He's so good with numbers, he ought to have a degree and be at some big accounting firm in Sacramento instead of doing the books for all these rinky-dink places in town. When I got out of high school I was determined not to go to Cosumnes or Valley or any other junior college, but to go right to Sac. State. And there was no way I was going to commute."

She took a long drink of her beer and continued, "Look, I love this place. It's been my family's home for seventy years. I get why people would want to live here, but sometimes, you know, I think the reason people are down here is because they're afraid. Afraid of people who don't look like them or think like them. Afraid they will be exposed as hicks if they go

45

beyond the city limits. So they stay down here on the river and double down on being what they're afraid of being, if that makes any sense. I don't even care that I never finished college. I'm goddamn proud I tried."

She took another pull of her beer and smiled at me. It was too dark in the truck to see her smile, but I could feel it. "How's that for speechifying?"

"Amen, sister," I said and saluted her with my beer.

"I love this place, I really do. But I'm tired of seeing people determined to repeat the past. So tell me right now, before I fall in love with you, if you're too chicken shit to try new things."

"I've been called a lot of things, but never a chicken shit."

"I don't mean being tough enough to take a punch."

"I know what you meant."

I let three curves pass before I answered, just so she'd know I didn't feel the need to jump at her every request. "I lived in Reno for three years, didn't I?"

She nodded.

"Falling in love with me, eh?"

"Don't get cocky, or I'll make you sleep at your parents' house tonight."

Things between us sped up from there. If I didn't get home too late from work I went over her house for dinner, and weekends became a standing date. Oh, sure, I still went fishing or shooting with Ray, but made sure I ended the day with Kathy. We had friends over her house for margaritas and I'd fire up the barbecue. After, we'd walk to Fred's and dance in the corner by the dartboard. I took some ribbing from Ray, and especially my dad, but I didn't care. I'd just smile and nod when they teased me about being pussy whipped. It felt good to give in to something, to not always be on the lookout for a fight that might or might not be coming my way. Those first six months with Kathy felt like those summer days when I was a kid and me and my brother would float down the river on inner tubes, letting the river carry us where it wanted. We'd get out at a friend's house, or stop and play on one of the islands every so

46

often. The day seemed to last forever and everywhere the river took us was a joyful adventure.

Work was slow again the next winter and Kathy suggested I see what the union had going on.

"You know how much I hate fucking unions," I said.

"You say that, but the union held your job for you when you were in jail, and it was union wages that bought that truck your daddy uses."

I knew I must have been in love with her because everything she said got through to me. I heard not only everything she said but everything she meant. No subject she brought up, or the manner she brought it up pissed me off, and I couldn't ever remember that being the case with anyone before.

"Just give yourself more options," she said. "You don't have to take the work if your daddy needs you, but if he doesn't, it's there for you."

I smiled. "You must be a helluva office manager."

"Why do you say that?"

"'Cause you are great at getting people to do what you want and making it seem like it was their idea."

She put her hands on her face in fake shock. "My secret is revealed. I'll have to kill you now. Why don't you come over here and let's see if I can fuck you to death."

When I told my dad I was going to see what work the union had, he just smirked and said, "Oh, yes, indeed. Pussy makes the world go round and round."

"Don't worry, our jobs still come first," I said.

"Pussy, pussy, pussy," my dad replied.

Soon I was working six days a week. Between the jobs my dad had and union work, I was all over the Sacramento area: Folsom, Woodland, Roseville, Davis, El Dorado Hills. Some nights I would crash at the Motel Six nearest to the job site instead of driving back down to the Delta.

Kathy didn't mind. She knew Sacramento better than I did, and sometimes when I would call her to tell her I'd be staying over, she'd say something like, "Oh, that Motel Six is next to the Embers. Well, if you go for a lap dance tonight, make sure you get a good looking girl. You deserve it."

She'd say things like that, and I would have to stop myself from blurting out something stupid like, "Marry me!" For the first time I started keeping a budget of what I made and what I spent. I even added a new category: money I kept. Every paycheck I tried to push more and more into that third category.

Rain came at the end of winter, in amounts the area hadn't seen in thirty years. One storm brought two inches of rain for four straight days, another dumped four inches in one day. Levees all over the Delta were overwhelmed, not breaking with one great flourish but instead by one crack leading to another crack until every rice farm in a twenty-mile radius was under water. The causeway that separated Stanton from Sacramento was filled and didn't recede until April. The bridge over the causeway was low, and, with it as full as anyone could ever remember, it appeared as if the water never ended. And when the wind kicked up, the causeway was as choppy as any ocean. Every night on the news there was a picture of some creek unable to contain all of its water, or some overwhelmed drain system.

Down river a few miles from town, so many trees fell over into the water a dam was almost created. Long thick roots, pounds of earth still stuck to them, poked out of the river turned brown from all the mud that couldn't hold itself to the bank. Around town, in between jokes about building an ark or seeing animals lined up two by two, people started telling each other, for the first time I could ever remember, to be careful when they drove the river road. It didn't help. Todd Peterson hydroplaned off the road right into June Stuckey's garage, Shorty Mitchell came around a corner and ran smack into a tree that had fallen across the road and Sandy Bloom's car stalled going through a puddle and old man Noyes rear-ended her.

With so many trees down, we could see the back end of my uncle's house before the bend in the river took away our view.

48

He loved to sit under the cover of his back porch and smoke a cigar and drink whiskey straight out of the bottle. During the biggest storms we'd watch him from our living room, the red glow from the tip of his cigar like a light tower's beacon.

"Not even enough sense to come out of the rain," my mom would say under her breath. "I won't be surprised if he drowns himself from staring up at it."

"Isn't it cold out there?" I asked him.

"Water and time can create and destroy anything," he said. "To be able to witness that up close, you have to be willing to sacrifice."

Through the winter and spring, because of the union, I still had work. A job would be shut down for a week because of a storm and we'd have to work twelve hours on a Saturday and Sunday to make up for it, but it was nice not to have to hibernate for three months, to be able to go out for dinner on Friday night with Kathy, or to plan a vacation for the summer because the money for it was already in the bank. We bought a house that spring after we got our tax refunds. It was a little two-bedroom starter home in what passed for the main part of town. I never thought I'd live where I couldn't see the river from my front door, but I wasn't complaining.

Our friends thought we were moving too fast. You could tell by the way they'd ask how long we'd been dating, things like that. All I knew was that for the first time since my brother died I could see a future there on the Delta. When I told my parents about buying the house and moving in with Kathy, my mom smiled approvingly and my dad said, "You just gotta bull rush everything, don't you, son?"

"If it ain't broke," I said.

"Well, she owns half of you now," he said.

"She has her own money," I said. "We're partners on the house."

"I wasn't talking about the house, son."

He came by a few weeks later saying he wanted to go fishing. "Let's go to the Yuba," he said.

"In case you haven't noticed, we live kinda close to a river," I said.

"A man can't fish the same hole his entire life, boy. It'll spoil his rod."

"If you got something to say, say it old man."

"Me? I'm just talking about fishing."

"Yeah, you're about as subtle as a kick in the nuts."

We drove the hour and a half to the Yuba River and fished till the early afternoon, catching three each. There had been so much water the past winter that the bend we normally fished on had moved thirty yards. We came upon it just past the empty gravel pit a half-mile off the road. Usually once we got to the gravel pit we could smell the water, feel it in the air, but that day we saw it.

"Holy shit," I said. "Have you ever seen it like this?"

My dad shook his head. "Don't fuck with mother nature," he said.

After lunch we set our beer cans on some rocks and took turns shooting my dad's .38 pistol at them.

"I need you week after next," my dad said.

"Yeah? How's it feel to need?" I said, a line he used to give me and my brother whenever we asked for something. He'd say, do you want it or need it, and if we said we wanted it, he'd say we could do without. If we said we needed it, he'd give us that line.

"Don't be a smart ass."

"For how long?"

"Two weeks. Better make it three. It takes a whole week to get you to stop working like a union member and get anything done."

I smiled. I'd rather have my dad half-drunk busting my balls than full-on drunk roaming from room to room looking to bitch at someone for reasons he only knew.

"You better be nice to me or I'll keep working those union jobs and make you work with Uncle Wayne."

My dad snorted. "I tell you what, I think he's crazy about full-time now. Seems we can't go more than a day without getting pissed off at each other."

"Just like an old married couple."

"Listen to you. Banging the same woman for a year doesn't make you an expert on anything, son."

That was the thing with my old man. He could always give it but only sometimes take it. The problem is, I always had a hard time figuring out what mood he was in or what caused it to change. "Is he drinking too much?" I asked.

"That and on all sorts of happy pills: uppers, painkillers, antibiotics, you name it. He makes his own little concoctions and swallows them down with a shot of Jack. When you try to ask him exactly what he's taking he mumbles something then changes the subject."

"That's too bad."

"We had some times, me and your uncle."

"Yeah?"

"Then he went off to Nam and when he came back I was dating your mother and nothing was ever quite the same. You know, I've never understood that," my dad continued, "the way guys get all bent out of shape if one of their buddies goes out with their sister. I mean, no one wants to think of someone diddling their sister, but if a guy is good enough to be your friend, who else would you want dating your sister?"

"Think he'll ever get better?"

"I doubt it. I hope so. Either way, life goes on."

He emptied his gun on a defenseless Budweiser can, sending it skipping along the ground. "Well, now that you've woken up all the fish, let's go get some of them," I said.

We waded out to where the river had been before the storms. We were in tennis shoes and jeans. All those years of having the Sacramento River as our backyard made the coldness of the Yuba irrelevant. This Yuba River, though, was unlike the one we fished the year before. It dropped off steeply where it used to begin, the new water cutting a deep path through the soil in search of a new home. The current became stronger with every step. My dad slipped and went under for a moment.

"Motherfucker," he yelled as he came up, whipping his head around to get the hair out of his eyes.

"I thought you were going to sleep with the fishes there for a second," I said. "What happened?"

"The ground just disappeared underneath me. Man, this must've been something to see at the height of all the flooding."

We fished for the better part of an hour without talking, moving up river together, casting out and reeling in. The wind picked up and it became clear the best of the fishing was over for the day, but neither of us said anything. We had nowhere to be except on the river.

"Kathy," my dad said, "she knows all about your scrapes with the law, the jail time? She's okay with it?"

I walked over to him because the wind was making it hard to hear. I had to kick my knees up out of the water because of the current. "Hell," I said when I got near him, "everyone in town knows about it."

He nodded. "True, true. It's just that sometimes all people look at is the result, not what caused it."

"She just doesn't want me getting in any more trouble, going forward," I said.

"No woman does. The problem is what they consider trouble and what we consider trouble usually ain't the same thing."

"I ain't ashamed of any of it," I said. "I was just trying to deal with shit the best way I knew how. Just 'cause it wasn't the smartest way, don't make me an asshole."

"I'm glad you think that way," my dad said and cast his line. "I mean, you're an asshole for a whole lot of other reasons."

"Mostly from traits I inherited from my old man," I said.

We stood and fished, not bothering to move. "I guess I should tell you," my dad said, "You're not the only one in the family who didn't handle things too smart."

"What do you mean?"

"It was right before you moved back. It was a Friday during football season and I saw a kid from school with his jersey on, you know how they wear them to school on game day?"

52

I nodded.

"I didn't even know him, and he didn't look like your brother or anything, but something about it got to me. Without any pads on the jersey hung down almost to his knees and off his shoulders halfway down his arms. It made him look like a child but whose childhood was gone, if that makes any sense."

He looked at me but I could tell he didn't expect me to say anything, which was good because I had no idea what to say except that I understood completely.

"Anyway, you can probably guess the rest. I got shitfaced and got a DUI, a little resisting arrest and assaulting an officer."

"Franklin?" I asked.

My dad shook his head. "Nah, that new deputy. Watts, I think, is his name."

"Only one DUI?" I said. "You're an amateur."

"It's nothing to joke about, for Christ's sake. What if I had hurt somebody?"

His implication should've shamed me but it only pissed me off. But it was my dad so there was a certain level of meanness in his reply that I had to let be. I mean, what was I going to do, go to blows with my old man? Instead I went for the joke. "Don't worry, if you drive anything like you fish, you were in no danger of hitting anyone."

He shook his head like I was the biggest asshole in world.

As we started home my dad said, "Your mother thought I was too tough on your brother after the accident. But I was trying to get him to see that it was an accident and not his fault."

He was looking out at the road, gripping and re-gripping the steering wheel. "He never came around to see it that way. He just…never came around," he said, his voice trailing off.

There was a big lip where the dirt road met the main road and we hit it too fast and at a wrong angle. The next thing I knew we were upside down and skidding across the road. I crawled out the window but between the beer and smacking my head on something in the truck, I was dizzy enough that I had to remain sitting. I felt my head. There was no blood but a bump was already forming above my eyebrow.

"Dad?" I said.

"Over here."

I crawled over to the driver's side. "You okay?"

"Help me out," he said. "I got my foot caught under the clutch. It's twisted up pretty good."

I pulled him out and leaned him up against the truck. Except for his ankle he looked fine.

"The road just jumped right up on us, didn't it?" he said.

"Truck seems fine," I said.

"Other than being upside down?"

"Think anyone will notice?" I said.

"Why don't you gather up all the beer cans and throw them in the grass across the road."

As I was doing that, two cars stopped and asked if we were all right.

"That lip is a motherfucker, ain't it?" one of them said. "I popped a tire on it once. I complained to the county but they said they wouldn't do anything about it until someone got hurt."

"Well, that ain't us," my dad said. "If you can help us get the truck upright, we'll be on our way."

"If you need to get going," the man said as we tipped the truck over, "I'd get going. I called the sheriff when we first pulled up."

My dad's eyes narrowed like if he had a few extra minutes he wouldn't have minded kicking that guy's ass. The man sensed it because he said, "I didn't know if it was a bad accident or not."

The pistol had slid out from under the seat. "Make sure it's not loaded and stuff it behind the seat," my dad said.

The truck hesitated, then started, but before my dad could put the truck into gear, we saw a Yuba County Sheriff coming toward us. He was probably still over a mile away, but the road

54

was flat and if we saw him, he was sure to have already seen us sideways on the wrong side of the road. There was no point in trying to run. We stepped out of the truck without a word. I was strangely calm watching him come toward us even though I knew there was not much good that could come out of this encounter. It was like he was coming for us in slow motion.

"Listen, son," my dad said, "I can't take another drunk driving so close to the first one. Especially with all that other shit tagged on to it."

"Who can?" I said.

"You've had less to drink than me, you're probably under the limit. "

"I'm also on probation."

"If you're over the limit they'll just extend it again. Same as the other times."

"If it's no big deal, why don't you take it?"

"Who the hell's going to look after your mom if I go away? I've got all those jobs lined up. You going to quit the union and finish them with that new house payment of yours? You can do the work but you've never run a business."

"I can't fucking believe this," I said.

"Do this for me, son. Please. I'll make it up to you, don't worry."

"I love you dad, but for the record, you're a motherfucker."

"Hey, now, watch your mouth!"

"Or what, you'll kick my ass?"

"It's an option."

The sheriff pulled up and gave a quick burst of his siren to get our attention. "Everyone okay?" he asked as he stepped out of his car.

My blood alcohol content was .08, just over the legal limit. Of course.

Kathy hung up on me when I called her from jail. I sat in that cell for two days and had to call Ray for a ride home when I was released. There was no way I was calling my dad for anything.

When I walked through the front door Kathy stood up from the kitchen table and went into our bedroom and locked the door. The few times in my life I'd had to apologize had ended badly. I'd start saying all the right things but underneath my anger would settle in on me like tule fog. I thought people expected an apology for every little thing and that they ought to have thicker skin, or I would be mad at myself for having screwed up so royally. Either way, my anger would finally overwhelm my words and the apology would turn into a fight.

I took a deep breath and walked slowly down the hall to our bedroom.

"Kat," I said, "I know you're mad, but if you let me explain, I think you'll see it differently."

"I'm not mad. I'm disappointed."

"Same difference."

"No," she said and came to the door. The shadow of her feet stretched out under the bottom of the door. "There's a big difference. A massive difference. A gargantuan difference. A motherfucking Grand Canyon of a difference," she said evenly.

"Okay," I said. "I get it. I fucking get it."

I walked away.

"Are you still there," she said through the door.

"Yeah," I said, coming back down the hallway.

"I wasn't driving, Kat. I know better than that. It was my dad who wrecked the truck. But he got a DUI a little while ago, and some other heavier shit. Assaulting a cop. I had only had a couple of beers, so I said I was driving. It was just dumb luck that I was over the limit. I mean, one tenth of one percent and we aren't even having this conversation."

"Whose idea was it?"

"His." I knew she wouldn't like my answer, but if you can't be honest to the woman you hoped to marry someday, what was the point of being together?

The door jerked open. "Are you fucking kidding me?" she yelled. "We've got this house, this life..."

"It's my dad. He asked."

56

"When you told me you were in jail, I thought you were the dumbest shithead I'd ever heard of. Now I think you're dumb for a whole other reason."

"Jesus Christ, Kat."

"What the hell else am I supposed to say? I'm not surprised that your dad asked you to take the hit for him, being father of the year and all."

"All right, that's enough of that shit!" I had to move to try to get some of the anger out of my system. I stomped back down the hallway towards the kitchen, slamming shut the half-open door of the bathroom and the spare bedroom.

"Let's keep this between the two of us or shit's going to get real ugly real fast," I said.

Kathy followed me to the kitchen. She put her hands on both sides of my face and turned me to her. If it had been any other person in the whole world who had done that, they would've gotten a fist in return.

"This is what you're going to do, sweetheart. Tomorrow we are going to drive to the sheriff's office and tell them the truth and get out from under this mess."

"They've already got my blood, baby. The charge is in the books. I've got a probation hearing in a month. There's no getting out from under anything."

"Then we'll fight the hell out of it. You have access to legal help through the union right? And you've got some money in your 401K, right?"

"I don't think it'll come to that."

"I don't want you doing any time," she said. "I can't stand the thought of it."

And then she was crying, head pressed tight against my neck, and all my anger washed away.

The flaw in my dad's plan was that I was a felon and there was a weapon in the truck. I hadn't thought of it either, which was my fault. I had given up my concealed weapon permit like the court ordered, but still went out duck hunting with my uncle or would shoot rattlesnakes and rabbits along the river road while driving around with Ray. It was what we had always done and I saw no reason to stop just because I had been caught drinking and driving too much.

I was given a year in Folsom Prison. It wasn't like the Johnny Cash song. Most of the real bad-asses were sent down to Pelican Bay, but still, it was no fun. Nothing bad happened to me, but the stress that something might happen will eat a man up. I thought of my brother during many a restless night in my cell. It was guilt that drove him crazy, no doubt, but I think it was realizing that his world was reduced to an eight by eight cell with no end in sight that led him to kill himself. I had a date in my head when I would get out and a job and a woman to get back to, and still the stress almost got to me.

Kathy came for a conjugal visit halfway through my stretch. It was both great and disappointing, if you can imagine that. It's hard to let your guard down after being on high alert for six months. At the end of the weekend she told me she was behind on the house payment.

"Talk to my dad," I said. I understood why she waited till the end to bring up business but I still didn't want to deal with it.

"I did. He gave me some money, but that was for last month."

"I thought he had a bunch of jobs going on?"

"A couple of the contractors haven't paid him yet. And I guess your uncle is all kinds of crazy nowadays so he's had to hire more people to pick up the slack. They've gotten into it a couple of times now, real fist fights."

"It's been heading that way for a while now," I said. "Can you hang on until I get out?"

"We'll see," she said and I could tell by the flatness of her voice that I wasn't the only one doing time.

"Hey, babe. This weekend was great and all, but I don't want you thinking you have to come see me every weekend."

"What are you talking about? I don't mind."

"I know, and I love seeing you, but this is my stretch. You don't have to do it with me," I said.

58

"I want us to do everything together, or haven't you been listening to me for the past year?"

"I know, I know. But this is my screw up, let me carry it."

"Even if I'm not here, I'm here," she said. "So I might as well be here."

We sat and stared not at each other, but over and next to each other, for a few long minutes. I gathered myself, determined to not let prison take my entire life, to not let all the bad luck of my past contaminate my future.

"Listen, Kat. I'm sorry. For everything. Once I get out I'll get back to work with the union and make some real money. I won't ever sniff trouble again."

She smiled, patted my hand and kissed me on the cheek. To this day I don't know if she believed me. I suspected she had begun not believing in me, but at that moment I couldn't let that doubt into my head.

With little over a month to go before getting out, I was summoned to the warden's office. It was either going to be something really bad or really good, I knew that. You don't go to the warden's office to shoot the shit.

"Your father is dead," he said before my ass had even touched the seat.

"He was stabbed," he continued when I didn't say anything. "By your uncle."

I felt like I was underwater. Everything seemed to be moving slow and was out of focus. "Where?" I managed to ask though I could barely hear the words come out of my mouth.

"During a fight at your parents' house."

"No, where on his body?"

"In the chest." He looked down at the papers in front of him. "With a butcher knife. Your uncle is being held in county jail pending charges."

He came around the desk to where I was sitting and held out his hand. I shook it without much thought or grip.

"You'll be allowed to attend the funeral. I'll let you know when I have more details. Sorry for your loss."

Kathy came to see me the next day. "I'm so sorry, babe. How are you doing?"

I had spent the night screaming into my pillow, anger and pain howling out of me, regret and guilt filling the empty space in my heart. I shrugged, started to say something and instead, shrugged again.

"Do you want to talk about it?"

"I'm not trying to be a jerk or anything," I said, my voice a whisper, "but I don't know what there's to talk about, Kat. It's done and there ain't no undoing it."

"I can't believe it. I didn't believe it when your mom called me and I still can't believe it as we're here talking about it."

"Well, it's real enough for my dad. And soon it'll be real enough for my uncle."

"What's that mean?"

"You know what that means, Kat."

"No, I really don't."

"When I get out of here I'm going to kill that sonofabitch."

"And end up right back in here?"

I shook my head. "I'm going to do him like he did my dad. I'll pick a fight with him then stab him right in the fucking heart."

Kathy didn't say anything for a long time. I stared at my hands. "I know you're hurt," she said finally, her voice flat and low. "Take a deep breath and you'll be out of here before you know it. We'll get a place in Sacramento or anywhere you want, and we'll put all this behind us."

I nodded. "That all sounds great Kat. But first I'm going to kill him."

"Stop talking like that."

"Okay." Now it was my voice that was calm and certain.

"Stop thinking like that," she said.

"I wish I could."

"I can't sit here and listen to this," she said and stood to go.

"How's my mom?" I asked.

"She needs you home."

I nodded.

"Your uncle's a wreck, in case you were wondering."

"I wasn't," I said, and Kathy turned and walked away.

Two days later, a day before my dad's funeral, a letter came from Kathy. She wouldn't be going to the funeral and wouldn't be coming to see me anymore. She had moved out of our house and was living with a friend in Sacramento. The bank was ready to start proceedings to take the house and if I wanted it I would have to act quickly. She said she knew writing a letter was a chicken shit way to end it with me, but that if she tried to do it in person she might not be able to see it through, and all that would do was delay the inevitable. It all turned out to be too much, but she wouldn't apologize for that. I love you. I'll always love you, she wrote. She ended the letter with some bullshit fortune cookie advice: Put yourself first more often.

I threw the letter right away. I was determined not to sulk around and read it and reread it until I was so angry at her that I went after someone inside. A month to go and I'd be damned if I was going to spend one extra day inside a cell. Besides, I had a plan to get her back. See, it was never anything between the two of us, it was all the other shit going on in my life that tripped us up. When my time was up I'd finish any work my dad had going on, then go back to the union. I'd already decided to let our house go. No use digging into my retirement to keep a bunch of wood and nails she didn't care about. I'd take every job the union had and get us a bigger house, even move out of the Delta if that's what she wanted. After I made things right with my uncle.

I'd never thought much about what I wanted in life. I figured to have as much fun and take as little shit as possible before my time was up. But now I wanted something. I needed something. And my dad be damned, it felt good to need. I figured it would take about six months before the time would be right to reach out to Kathy.

Fred gave my dad's eulogy. Any other situation and it would have been my uncle giving it. Two sheriffs drove me to the cemetery and waited by their unmarked car. I had on an ankle bracelet and a charcoal suit my mom bought for me. I looked around for Kathy but she wasn't there, and I felt a little guilty for thinking of her at my dad's funeral.

Fred started by saying he had a lot of stories about my dad but didn't know if all of them could be told in mixed company. Everyone laughed knowingly. He told a few of the tamer ones I'd heard a dozen times then finished by saying, "He was a tough man who did a tough job. He could be hard at times, but deep down he was a good man. He didn't stand for a lot of B.S., though he liked nothing better than to have a few beers and B.S."

People laughed and Fred said, "Am I right?" and people laughed some more.

"Anyway, he knew what it meant to be the head of a family and the tough love that can be a part of it. Yes sir, underneath that gruff exterior was a good heart, and I'm going to miss him."

I thought that summed up my old man pretty well. I closed my eyes tight against the tears and pressed my fingers against the edges of my eyes to hold them inside. I opened my mouth wide, trying to stretch my jaw in order to relieve the tightness that was running from my lower back up through my shoulders and neck all the way to my jaw.

Fred asked if I wanted to say a few words. I nodded weakly and took my time walking to the front of the crowd. After that first night, I hadn't spent much time thinking about my dad's death. Prison is no place to let your emotions get the best of you, to run things round and round in your brain till your thoughts have no place to go but out into the world. I had spent the past seventy-two hours keeping my head down and mind closed. But now I owed it to my dad to speak.

I looked out at the crowd. Every face looking back at me was familiar. I'm no good at speaking without thinking about it beforehand, even though many say that's all I do and that's what leads to all my trouble. "My dad was the best fisherman I knew, probably the worst poker player I knew, and made the

62

best barbecued ribs I've ever had." It wasn't much, but it was the best I had in me at the moment.

The sheriffs took me to my parents' house so I could change out of my suit. My mom was at the kitchen table arranging all the cakes and pies that had been brought over. She hugged me, opened her mouth to say something, started to cry, and stopped. We hadn't talked about what had happened or what was going on with my uncle. I only had three hours to attend the funeral. There would be time for that when I got out.

I changed and went into the bathroom to take a piss in private for the last time in a month. I splashed water on my face and looked in the mirror at myself and started crying. Not loud sobs, but I couldn't stop the tears no matter how quickly I brushed them away. They kept coming and I felt my neck and shoulders loosen. My chest expanded and I breathed deeper than I had in a year. I welcomed the tears as the small of my back untightened and my hips unlocked. I looked at myself in the mirror again and smiled at my wet face. "I'll be goddamned," I said.

Ray came and got me when I was released. For just an instant I thought Kathy would be waiting inside his car to surprise me, but I quickly forced that thought out of my heart. My mom had never come to visit me any of the other times I was away. I understood and didn't blame her. There's a big difference between knowing someone has screwed up and having to see it. I took a long hot shower when I got home, laying on the floor of the tub until the water ran cold. After chomping at the bit for a year to get out and make my life right, I wasn't sure if I was up to it right that moment.

My mom called me into the kitchen where two shots of whiskey sat on the table.

"I should probably take it easy with that stuff," I said.

"I won't tell if you won't," she said.

"I don't know if getting out of prison is worthy of a celebration."

She downed her shot, one of the few times I could remember her drinking something other than beer. "I figure we got a lot to talk about, so let's get to it."

I sat down, tossed the whiskey to the back of my throat and about threw it back up.

"I know," she said as I coughed. "It's some rotgut, some store brand your dad got on sale a while back."

"Since you seem determined to not let me ease on back into anything, what's going on?" I asked when I got my breath back.

She poured two more shots. "Can I at least get a beer chaser?" I asked.

"Good idea," she said and reached into the refrigerator from her seat for two beers.

"Your uncle, he's not right."

"What was your first clue, the knife sticking out of dad's chest?"

"My brother," she began, then stopped and picked up her shot. "It all got to be too much for him: the war, the booze, the pills." She drank her shot and continued. "And your father, it seemed to make him mad, really mad, that his best friend wasn't the same anymore. Then to have to work together and see it every day."

"Who started it?" I asked. I didn't want to hear any psychological bullshit about why the fight happened. My dad was dead, and I wanted his death made right.

"Who knows?" she said, frustrated by my tone. "They were already shouting and in each other's face when I came home."

"Did you see him do it?"

She shook her head. "I was tired of seeing it. I went to my room." She pushed my shot closer to me. I took it without thinking.

"Your uncle is claiming self-defense. The district attorney is still deciding what to charge him with, third-degree murder or manslaughter or maybe even reckless endangerment."

"Shit, he's the crazy one. If anything, dad was probably defending himself against his craziness. Plus, he never could've taken dad in a fair fight. He knew he was going to use that knife." I drank my shot. "He fucking knew."

My mom was quiet for a long time. She stared out the window like she was thinking of all kinds of things, things that had

64

to do with our conversation and things that had nothing to do with it. Some, I was sure, were both.

"I've lost too much family," she said finally.

"I know."

"I'm going to testify for my brother."

It took me a second to realize what she was saying, and another second to believe it. "What the fuck are you talking about?" I said, my voice rising, the anger suddenly in my throat, my chest and shoulders tight like someone had me in a bear hug. "You didn't even see it."

"But I know the way he treated your uncle. I know the way he treated everyone. You think you're the only one he slapped on the back of the head?"

"That has nothing to do with this. He's your husband for Christ's sake!"

"And Wayne is my brother."

"You choose your crazy brother over your husband?"

"He's the one still here, don't you understand," she said, her voice breaking.

I stood and kicked my chair against the wall. "Well, let me tell you something, you choose him and you'll lose me. That's for goddamn sure."

"Listen to me, sonny boy," she said, her voice sturdy again, "you can get as pissed off as you want, but remember, your uncle and dad wouldn't have been on each other so much if you would've been around this past year."

It was like Sheriff Franklin had slapped me in the face all over again. "Are you kidding me? Wait. Are you fucking kidding me? I took that hit for him, for you."

"I never asked you to."

"No, but he did. Said he needed to take care of you. I lost my house and my girlfriend because of it, and now you have the fucking balls to sit here and tell me it was my fault!"

"No, I'm sorry. I shouldn't have said that. I'm just saying there has been a lot of shit that has happened to this family and I want to hold onto what's left of it."

"Yeah," I said, "you have a funny fucking way of showing it."

I went to Fred's and got blind drunk, calling Ray to pick me up as soon I got there. "I'll make a deal with you," Fred said when I walked in and he saw the look on my face. "I'll let you drink all the beer you want on the house, but no whiskey. Don't even ask me for it."

It was a Monday and the only other people in the bar were a couple of old alcoholics so I drank and drank until I woke up on Ray's couch.

"I want you staying with me for a while," he said.

I shook my head. "You don't have to worry about me doing something stupid," I said. I meant it. I just wanted to get back to work and get with Kathy and put the Delta in my rearview mirror.

"You say that now, but wait until this hangover goes away."

"Did I tell you she's testifying for my uncle against my dad?"

"That's all you talked about last night. I can't believe it. That's some crazy shit, buddy."

"They can have each other. I'm through with them."

I went to the union hall the next day and by the end of the week had been assigned onto a job. I took jobs all over Northern California—Chico, Redding—even back up to Reno. The farther away, the better. I took all the overtime offered to me, working my hands so hard calluses quickly came then disappeared, leaving knots of tissue and muscle under the skin. Any days I was in the area I either grabbed a hotel room or crashed on Ray's couch. I didn't see my mom for over a year. Ray told me my uncle had moved in with her after getting out of prison. Un-fucking-believable I said—but, of course, it was completely believable.

I didn't go to the trial, but Ray kept me informed as to how it went. My uncle pleaded self-defense and, sure enough, my mom lied on his behalf. He was found guilty of involuntary manslaughter and given two years with the chance to be home

66

in one with good behavior. Ray thought I was living the high life, traveling all over Northern California, having my meals and hotel room paid for instead of being stuck on the Delta helping his dad run the family business. It was a combination bait and liquor store with a boat motor repair shop in back, and the occasional truck, boat, and trailer for sale in the parking lot.

What I told Ray, but he never seemed to listen to, was that my per diem covered nothing more expensive than fast food and Motel Six. I don't know what he thought he was missing. I thought he had life by the balls. He was seeing a gal from Rio Vista, had fixed up the stores and they were making more money than they ever had. He was doing such a kick-ass job with the family business his dad signed over the rights to all the land and buildings and started working for Ray.

While out on a job, I'd go weeks with only seeing the job site or the inside of my motel room. I even stopped going to bars, though that didn't mean I'd stopped drinking. Three nights in a hotel room alone were all I could handle. Like clockwork, you could find me on that fourth night sitting on the bed watching some crap television show drinking whiskey out of those little plastic cups they leave in your room. I worked with a lot of Mexicans that year and the favorite word of theirs that I picked up was "*manaña*." It technically means "tomorrow," but it can also mean "not today." Almost every night I would think about calling Kathy. It had been over six months, and she would know that I hadn't killed my uncle—but I always put some excuse in my way: it was too late, I was too tired, I didn't have time for what would surely be a long and dramatic call. But the real reason I never called was that I wanted to be a better guy than the one she fell in love with, not a work in progress. I wanted to be in better shape, to be drinking less, to have more money in my pocket, to have less anger inside me. *Manaña*, I told myself. *Manaña*.

Nights I was drinking, I didn't even entertain a notion of calling her, knowing I wouldn't be able to hide the excitement of hearing her voice, or my anger if she wasn't just as excited to hear mine. When I talked to her it had to be with my head screwed on straight so we could really talk. Those nights I'd drink an ounce of whisky at a time and my mind would turn to all that had happened in my life, and how if I could have avoided just one or two of the crap things that had come my way, it would've made all the difference. I would feel weighed down the next day, and it would take me till lunchtime to find my groove. But I never drank two days in a row. I was determined to muscle my way through it all until I found a way forward.

I ran into Kathy one day in Old Town Sacramento. It had been almost a year and a half since I'd seen her. I was eating my lunch on a bench looking out at the river when I saw her come out of one of the more expensive restaurants in the city.

"Life must be treating you good, eating lunch at The Station," I said loudly.

She looked up, saw me, and smiled, which was nice. I brushed the dirt off my jeans as she crossed the road. "I wish," she said, standing in front of me. Her hair was longer than I'd ever seen it. I felt a little bit of adrenalin released into my body like just before a fight, but completely different. "I'm getting a gift certificate for my parents. It's their anniversary next week."

"How are they?"

"Good. Good."

"Do you want to sit down?"

"I have to get back to work."

"I thought you ran that place?"

"I do. That's why I have to be back."

"Of course." I wanted to tell her that I had thought of calling her a thousand times, but then I realized she had never called me.

"I saw your mom a while back," she said.

"She always liked you," I said.

"But she loves you." When I didn't respond she continued. "She told me what happened with the trial."

I nodded, my stomach tightening with each word she spoke. I rolled my neck in order to loosen it up. "You think I should forgive her, Kat?"

"I don't know. I just know you only have one mother, good or bad, right or wrong."

"And she only had one husband. And one son left."

She brushed her hair from one side of her head to the other, blocking the sun from my eyes. For months I had imagined what I'd say or do when I saw her again, how I'd bare everything to her, pledge everything for her. Instead, I just sat there, comforted by her presence. As sure as I knew my brother was gone that night on the river bank, as sure as I knew I had fallen in love with Kathy driving up and down the river road, I knew what we had was gone. I should have made it harder for her to leave me but I had miscalculated how much she wanted away from the Delta, and there was no going back to fix it. The past either sets the hook deep or not at all.

"Where are you working?" she asked.

"On the jail expansion on Twentieth Street. That's irony, right?"

She laughed. "I think so."

"Well," I said, standing, wanting to be the first to leave.

"Take care of yourself," she said.

"You were the best girlfriend I ever had, Kat."

"I was the only girlfriend you ever had," she said and we both laughed.

We were on the final push to get a job in Davis wrapped up. We worked ten hours a day and a full day on Saturday for the next two weeks. It felt good to be working so much.

On the second to last day of the job we were installing floor to ceiling interior plates of glass worth about nine hundred dollars each. It took three of us to set each one, me and a guy on each side and another on bottom telling us where to set it. We only had four to do that day so we took an early and long lunch, sharing a twelve pack of beer. As we were working the last one into place it slipped away from me, flipped up, hit the wall and broke. A piece shaped like a thunderbolt cleaved my shoulder.

Everyone on the job started yelling and rushing me to a truck to take me to the hospital, but I wasn't overly worried. No one ever died from a cut in the shoulder no matter how deep, and since it was still lodged in me, there wasn't too much blood to get worked up about. Everything was numb and I just leaned back while they drove me to the hospital in Sacramento. I opened my eyes a few times when we passed cars to see the flipped out look on the driver's face when they saw big hunk of glass sticking out of my shoulder.

The glass cut through every muscle in my shoulder, not missing a single one, if you can believe that. The tendon that connected the shoulder to the shoulder blade was severed for good measure. The doctors said it would take a while but I should be good as new eventually. It was three months after the surgery before I could start any type of rehab, and after six months of therapy my shoulder was still no good. They would stick me in a tub full of water and turn on the jets—hydrotherapy they called it—and try to rotate my arm, or get it to simply raise above my head, but it wouldn't. When they forced it into positions or angles it wasn't ready for, it hurt more than any punch I'd taken in a fight, and if they continued, the poor therapist got an earful of curses. Deep tissue massages left me in tears, which I would've gladly taken if they had helped. Outside of the rehab, the shoulder didn't give me much trouble as long as I let it linger by my side. It was only when I tried to make it do more than it was capable of that the pain would come, like a burst of electricity in and out of my arm for an instant, yet leaving behind hours of pain. I couldn't raise it above my head or back far enough to touch my back, which made combing my hair and wiping my ass an adventure.

The whole time that was going on I was either staying at Ray's—sneaking in and out of town before my mom knew I was around—or spending money for a motel in Reno or downtown Sacramento. The union sent me to three different doctors and they all said the same thing: The shoulder should be better but it wasn't. After almost two years of being stretched and poked at and X-rayed by doctors and therapists, I was declared permanently disabled.

I live now with my mom and uncle. I showed up one day with all my belongings in two duffel bags and she let me in. Me and my uncle have never talked about my dad's death. What's the point, we have to live in the same house together. Whenever he gets on my nerves or starts acting really goofy I take a walk down to the river or into town. I probably didn't deserve to have my mom open her door for me, but I knew she would. She's quieter than she used to be, yet quicker to lose her temper. Good thing yelling has never bothered me.

I drink too much. I try to hold off till noon each day but often lose that battle. I've gained weight, maybe fifty pounds. I saw Kathy a while back when she was in town visiting her family. I waved at her but she didn't recognize me.

Other than that, life isn't much different than when I was growing up here. I fish the same holes I did as a kid, take in the Friday night football games, hang out at Fred's, though I don't drink much when I go there because my disability check only pays me half of what I used to make, and plus I wouldn't be much of a fighter anymore with my bad wing. I don't see much of Ray. He married that Rio Vista girl and has a baby on the way. I have my old bedroom but usually sleep on the couch. After checking all the locks on the doors, I make a point of telling my mom that the house is all locked up. I like to fall asleep to the television while looking out at the river, waiting for the breeze to rise off it and carry the day away. Sometimes, in that moment before I'm asleep, before the cool air of the river has come to me, I wish that piece of glass had hit me in the heart instead of the shoulder. But I wasn't that lucky, I guess.

BUCK STEW

It was mid-January in Stanton, time for the Sportsman's Club's annual Buck Stew, and Jack Dixon was in the mood to get ugly. He was in the Oasis sipping on a beer, looking out the open front door at Highway 65 as it ran through town without hesitation. Everything was dry and brown with no promise of spring in the air. The bar was empty and the bartender was busy in the back taking inventory, leaving Jack alone with his beer and impossible-to-shake thoughts of Kristy. The beer, which he thought would be refreshing after last night's whiskey, was sour and flat. He had read once that on average it took one month to get over a breakup for every year a person had been in the relationship. Jack took another unpleasant taste of his beer and thought there was no way in hell he could last through another three months like the last two.

A train rumbled through town but they rarely stopped anymore since the feed store was on its last legs. After three generations of ownership, the Haswell family had sold it to a big agriculture company out of Sacramento that promptly laid off all the workers, then hired them back at reduced wages. Stanton people possessed two enduring qualities: loyalty to their neighbor and town, and an intense desire not to be fucked with. So the workers started shorting the bags of feed or not sewing the bags properly, until now the only customers left were the ranchers in Stanton, who got extra feed and grain in their orders so that the new owners would continue to lose money.

The highway remained vacant except for some locals passing by, like Nelson Stoker in his '57 Chevy with his two German shorthairs in back, and Angie Krentz in the Firebird she bought with the money she inherited from her mom. As Jack muscled down his beer no one new passed by, and, worse, he knew no one would. He decided it was time to take off when Al Flores' boy cruised by for the third time.

"Hey, Fred," Jack yelled, walking behind the counter of the bar. "I'm taking one for the road."

"Don't forget to leave a tip, you cheap bastard," Fred yelled back.

"I'll see you tonight, where they pour real drinks," Jack said, picking up the tip he had set down.

He started on a slow cruise around town, then decided not to waste his time and headed straight for home. He lived across the street from the backside of the Franklin-Martin plant and every time he pulled into his driveway he was thankful he didn't work there anymore. Stanton was hot enough, squatting in the middle of the Sacramento Valley, which began where the San Joaquin Valley stopped. No one knew exactly where the transition took place because both stretches of land were hot and flat and windy and never refreshing. If you worked at Franklin-Martin, or the Pottery as everyone called it, you were guaranteed to never escape the heat. Between the production of sewer pipe, brick, and roof tile, there were half a dozen kilns fired up at all times. The plant's metal buildings had tin roofs that allowed the heat from outside to pour down on the workers, and when a kiln was opened to push a car filled with product in or take one out, the wave of heat that rushed out made it near impossible to suck any air into your lungs.

Jack had worked in the sewer pipe division for ten years until getting laid off last year. All the years of contractors using inexpensive PVC pipe had finally caught up with the plant, and, even with ten years in, Jack was on the low end of seniority. He ran a one-man painting business now, but still used the plant's whistles throughout the day to gauge when it was time to get up, have lunch, or clean up and head for home.

He watched some cable, cleaned the kitchen, took a shower. He had spent the last two months pretty much the same way, marking the days in half-hour increments until it was time to go to sleep or start drinking. No matter what he did to push time over to the next day, hoping that would be the day it all got better, the urge to call Kristy had not dulled. But he vowed a dozen times a day not to call, and so far he hadn't.

Jack's neighbor, David Hicks, a three-time councilman who was involved in a runoff to determine who would be mayor, rolled up in his van and laid on the horn. Jack looked at his dull face in the kitchen window. "Let's have some fun tonight, for Christ's sake," he said.

David handed him a beer from a grocery bag on the seat between them as Jack climbed in the van. "Might need you to deal tonight," he said.

"What's wrong," Jack said, "can't find enough people in town who can count up to twenty-one?"

"Let's see, there's us two and about three others. That's five, isn't it?" David said, counting on his fingers.

"God damn piss-ass town," Jack said. He took a long drink of his beer. "I was kinda hoping to drink myself sloppy tonight."

"I wish you'd drink yourself into a piece of ass," David said. "Maybe then you'd quit moping around like a pup about to get whipped."

"Kinda tough at a stag party."

"With the luck you're having, you might want to consider switching sides."

"Fuck off," Jack said. He twisted in his seat away from David, rolled down the window and spit. "You don't know what the hell you're talking about. I haven't called Kristy once since we broke up."

"Hey, I was just making a friendly observation. No judgment involved."

Jack finished his beer and grabbed the final two from the grocery bag. "She was a bitch, wasn't she?" he said as he handed David a beer.

"Are you voting for me in April?"

"Of course."

"Then she was a total fucking ball-busting bitch," David said.

"That's what I thought," Jack said.

They touched beers and drank.

The Grange Hall was already full, so they drove around and parked in back. The headlights of the van swept over Tommy Sanchez pissing by his truck.

"Now that's what I call indecent exposure," Jack said as Tommy walked toward them.

"Jack fucking Dixon," Tommy said, zipping up. He looked at David and said, "You gotta start hanging out with a better class of people."

"That's what I keep telling him," David said, shaking Tommy's hand. "I can still count on your vote, right?"

"Now that you've asked for it, you can go fuck yourself," Tommy said.

Inside the hall, Jack bought twenty dollars' worth of raffle tickets and twenty dollars of drink tickets. He walked the room, stopping to talk with an uncle, a cousin, and an old friend of the family. He didn't know if it was the booze or the sight of familiar faces, but he felt relaxed, felt himself walking a little looser. Stanton was where he was; this was what he had. The town was easy to overlook. More than once Jack had been on a job in Sacramento and when he told people he was from Stanton they had no clue where it was, even though it was only thirty miles away. Like most of the people in town, he took pride in the fact that nothing had ever been handed to Stanton. Struggle might not be the prettiest thing to hang onto, but it was constant and Jack sincerely believed it was the only way to take on a world that was forever disappointing you in one way or the other. And, besides, nothing felt better than to kick the world square in the ass for ever doubting you. There would be David's Super Bowl party next weekend, the Portuguese Picnic in May, the Fourth of July party at the park, then hunting in the fall: deer, quail, and turkey. A year would pass before he knew it. He'd survive.

He ran into Tommy up at the bar. He was wearing a leather long rider jacket, and Jack wouldn't have been surprised if he had a gun hidden somewhere in it. They were the same age but Tommy looked at least five years older. Not in a bad way, but in an experienced way, like he had already gone through things Jack was just getting around to. "I can't believe you're still alive," Jack said to him.

"I'm sure half the fuckers in this room can't believe it either. That's why I like to come to these things, show these chair pussies how to live," Tommy said, rubbing his goatee to a point.

Jack tipped his beer to Tommy's. "If you need a running mate tonight, look me up." Jack had heard all the stories about Tommy: the fighting, the small-time drug running and pyramid schemes, but he also knew that when you hung out with him, sparks were bound to fly and he wouldn't mind being set on fire right about now.

After a dinner of buck stew, cheese bread, and box wine, the pornos started. Jack stood looking at the gyrations of the actors when David tapped him on the shoulder.

"Jesus Christ, act like you've seen one before," he said. "Come on, I need you on table three, pervert."

"I was just thinking," Jack said, "how that muff kinda looks like your wife's."

"Oh, shit," David said, clapping his hands. "The zombie awakens."

A few waitresses from the Kountry Kitchen Diner were working the event for tips, and Jack flagged one down and got a beer on the way to the blackjack table.

"Come on, boys, step right up," he said, shuffling the cards. He threw them around the table, pitching them high, inadvertently flipping a few over. "Feel free to take off both shoes if you need help counting up your cards."

Jack looked at the man playing first base. He didn't know him, which was odd for the Buck Stew. "Card?" he asked. The man waved him off, then Jack rapped twice softly and quickly on the felt and proceeded around the table.

Between hands, he sipped from his beer. He hadn't switched over to whiskey yet. Many a night lately had turned when he made the decision to go with whiskey instead of beer, turned from grief to anger, from despair to desperation.

Jack was winning three out of the five hands around the table almost every time. David was acting as pit boss and had the waitresses bring him a beer without even asking if he was ready. The pornos continued playing against the back wall of the hall: six-foot penises, vaginas the size of canoes, orgasms like shooting stars across the sky. The movies were old—the pictures crackled and light pierced through the split paneling of the wall. Jack and the players looked over between every deal. If the movies had had sound, the hands never would have gotten played.

The gambling was strictly low-key, dollar-minimum, five-maximum. Tommy and the old high school wrestling coach, Mr. Gardner, had been playing at the table for almost an hour straight, while the other three spots were never filled by one person for very long because Jack was winning so much.

"What do you say we raise the max to ten dollars," Tommy said.

"Why the hell not," Jack said. "In fact, I'll go you one better. Minimum is five bones."

Mr. Gardner lost five straight hands. He threw his cards down in disgust. "This ain't goddamn Vegas, you know." He used Tommy's shoulder to push himself up off his stool. "You would've been a helluva wrestler if you could've stayed healthy," he said to him. "Good balance, tough. A hundred sixty-five pounds, right?"

Tommy nodded.

"Yep. Too bad," he said, walking away.

Howie Baret, whose family owned the six hundred acres the Sportsman's Club leased, as well as a thousand-acre ranch they had run for three generations, sat down at first base. "Five bucks? Jesus Christ," he said.

"Quit bitching," Jack said. "Here's your chance to get some money of your own instead of waiting for your inheritance to kick in."

Jack kept winning and drinking. Howie played angry—and stupid—because of Jack's remark. He split a pair of tens then later doubled-down when Jack had an Ace showing. He lost close to a dozen hands in a row before play was shut down for the start of the raffle.

"No wonder Kristy dumped you," Howie said, walking away from the table.

The raffle started out small: John Deer hats, bottles of Early Times, Budweiser lamps. Then it was on to boxes of shotgun shells, a free dinner at the Depot, a free alignment and rotation at Hal's Tire Shop, and a year's worth of haircuts and shaves at Bill and Lupe's barbershop. The grand prize was a Glock handgun. Jack was in the bathroom by himself, swaying in front of the trough when he heard his name called.

"Do I need to sign any papers or anything?" he asked when David handed him the gun.

"Papers?" David said.

"Registration, transfer of ownership."

"Jesus Christ, Jack. How long have you lived in Stanton?"

The gambling was over. Jack's table cashed out at more than six hundred dollars on the plus side, as much as the other five tables combined. David slid a twenty-dollar bill in Jack's palm like he was the slyest politician who had ever lived. "Here's a little appreciation," he said.

The bar had begun to run out of beer. The kegs were dry, and all of the whiskey had been swallowed. They were down to vodka and lukewarm Pabst left over from a wedding reception a month ago. Jack walked the room again, bitter now because most of these men would be going home to wives or girlfriends. He heard talk of finishing off the night at the Oasis. He walked outside, not knowing what he wanted to do, but knowing that returning to the Oasis was not it. He pulled the Glock from his waistband and pointed it at the moon. He had gotten drunk tonight, but not ugly. He walked to David's van and pissed on the back tire.

"Shake it more than twice and you're playing with it," Tommy said from the shadows.

"What are you doing out here?" Jack said. "Waiting to roll someone?"

"Nah. Just had to puke," he said, tucking his ponytail into his jacket.

"You going to the O?" Jack asked.

"It's either that or go home and whack off. And I'm too drunk to do that," Tommy said and spit quickly three times.

"Let's head up the hill," Jack said.

"Reno?"

"Gamble some, then go whoring," Jack said.

"You got any stake?" Tommy asked. "I'm fairly tapped."

Jack felt the twenty-dollar bill in his pocket and knew it was not nearly enough. "I know where we can get some."

They drove out past Doddy's Ravine, left on Karchner, and up Gold Hill Road to Kristy's house on the top of the hill. Tommy charged up the hill with his lights off, bouncing from one side of the dirt road to the other.

"Shit. Could you go any faster?" Jack said.

"It's my theory that when you're committing a felony, you ought to get done with it as quickly as possible," Tommy said.

The lights were out in the house and Kristy's car was gone. Tommy turned the car around so it was facing back down the hill. "You sure about this?" he asked Jack.

"She's taken a lot more from me," Jack said.

The front door was unlocked, as he knew it would be. Jack didn't need any lights to find his way down the hall and to the top drawer of her dresser. He put his hands into socks and underwear that were so familiar, working his way through them until he felt the envelope. He grabbed it and walked quickly out of the house, his heart pumping, his hands clutching the envelope tighter with each step.

He nodded at Tommy when he reached the car. "I gotta piss real quick," he said.

"Tie a fucking knot in it," Tommy said, but Jack unzipped anyway. He turned away from Tommy but heard him tapping the steering wheel impatiently. Stanton wasn't much more than four thousand people—but from up on the hill, with all of its lights on display on a Saturday night, it looked much larger, more alive. Kristy was out there, Jack thought, somewhere in those lights, probably making someone laugh, making someone excited, making someone hope.

82

Jack finished and Tommy put the car in gear. "Hold up," Jack said.

"What the fuck now? You gonna write her a note?"

Jack shoved the clip into the Glock and fired it right through the huge living room window. It crumbled like sand hit by a wave. He then shot out the bedroom window and the glass on the front door.

"I love a man who doesn't do things halfway," Tommy said, clapping. "Now don't forget to pick up the casings."

They bought a six-pack of beer at the 7-Eleven in Auburn, then drove an hour and a half to the Peppermill on the south side of Reno.

"Best looking cocktail waitresses in town," Tommy said. "Thighs to their eyes."

They stumbled around until they found a blackjack table with two openings. It was a twenty-five-dollar-minimum table. Tommy sat down, but Jack hesitated.

"Please don't tell me we came all the way up here to play the two-dollar tables," Tommy said.

"Fuck you," Jack said. The envelope he had stolen from Kristy's had nine hundred dollars in it. He peeled off a C-note and handed it to Tommy. He slapped down another C-note for his first bet.

He lost the first hand, switched to betting twenty-five dollars at a time, and won the next three. They ordered cocktails. Tommy lost his first three hands, doubling his bet each time, a sucker's bet Jack knew, but still he kept giving Tommy money when he asked for it. Tommy won his fourth hand with eight hundred dollars out on the table. They high fived each other and touched glasses, spilling some of their drinks on the table. The dealer, Jasmine from Flagstaff, Arizona, stopped shuffling and looked at them.

As they played, others from the table left, aggravated with their loud, constant chatter, but after almost blowing all their money and getting it back, they felt invincible.

"We keep on winning like this, and we'll have us a hall of fame night at the Ranch," Tommy said.

Jasmine looked up at them again. "You'd better hurry. They're closing it in a week."

"What? Why?" Tommy cried.

"The IRS finally caught up to Colanari," she said.

"That's a damn shame," Tommy said. He and Jack toasted to a great American whorehouse.

Jack was blasted, the lights of the casino highlighting the harshness of his drunk. His eyes were red, his face heavy, his body bloated. He was ready for bed, but Tommy had his second wind due to the line of coke he had snorted in the bathroom. The only way Jack could think of to keep pace was to drink more. He ordered a shot of tequila with his next cocktail.

He stared at his chips. Between him and Tommy they had about eight hundred dollars out on the table. He had been squirreling away Kristy's money and now almost the same amount he had stolen from her sat in his front pocket. If he stopped now he could go over to her house tomorrow, act surprised and shocked at the shot-out windows, ask to use her bathroom, and sneak the money back into the dresser drawer.

But he didn't see what good that would do him. It would mean that tonight had just been an exercise, a dry run that would leave everything unchanged, and he had already had too many nights the past two months that had come to nothing but regret.

He slapped Tommy on the shoulder. "Come on, man. Let's go get some pussy."

The dealer looked up, rolled her eyes. "Oh, give me a break, sweetheart," Tommy said. "You don't want a piece of us, so we're going where we're wanted."

"Come on," Jack said, pulling Tommy away from the table.

"I mean, if you want, darling, I'll come back after I'm done out there and let you have a go at me."

"What the hell are you doing?" Jack said.

"She thinks she's such fucking hot stuff. Fuck her," Tommy said as they walked away.

84

A security guard was watching them, standing in the corner with his meaty arms across his chest. "Look the other way you fat fuck before I stick these chips up your ass," Tommy said. The guard spoke into his walkie-talkie.

"Jesus Christ, let's just get out of here," Jack said. He hustled Tommy out of the casino and into his car. They headed out to the Mustang Ranch, seven miles east of Reno.

"I'm gonna get me a big lipped, buck toothed gal and get a blowjob that'll curl my toes," Tommy said. "How about you?"

"Something different," Jack mumbled. "A black girl, or an Asian. I gotta have someone different."

They were silent for a few minutes, then, as they exited off I-80 to the Mustang, Tommy looked at Jack. "That old fucker was right, you know. I could've been a good wrestler. But no *cojones,* no *corazón.* No fucking *cojones.*"

"You were unlucky with injuries, that's all," Jack said.

"No. I could've wrestled through 'em. They gave me an excuse not to go onto the mat, and I took it. I didn't care about getting beat up. I didn't want to get beat."

"How'd you grow 'em?" Jack asked.

"What?"

"*Cojones.* You sure got 'em now."

"Maybe I'm just doing a better job of pretending," Tommy said.

"No," Jack said. "I know when somebody's faking."

Jack grabbed the Glock as they pissed outside the car in the parking lot. He readjusted it in his waistband and pulled his coat over it as Tommy pressed the buzzer at the entrance of the Mustang. The gate unlocked and they walked to the front door. Jack touched the gun as they walked. Its weight was awkward, pulling his pants down on his waist.

They opened the front door and were met by seven women standing at attention, waiting to be picked. One wore hot pants, two had on low-cut dresses, and the rest were packed into brightly colored spandex exercise outfits. All seven of the women were white.

"Looks like you're going to have to re-evaluate your choice," Tommy said. He stepped ahead of Jack towards the bar. "Come on, first round's on me."

A thin, pale redhead in line made eye contact with Jack, and he held out his hand and they walked down the hall to her room. "My name's Desiree," she said.

"Jack." His mouth was dry and he was sure he was slurring.

She sat on the bed, her dress bunching up high on her thighs. She wasn't wearing underwear and Jack was happy that she appeared to be a true redhead. The world's false enough without people lying about the color of their hair, he reasoned.

"Well, Jack," she said. "What are you in the mood for? Half and half, a threesome, the Jacuzzi room, around the world?"

"Any going out of business specials I should know about?"

She laughed. "Not yet."

"Half and half, then." He smiled weakly. "Nothing too exciting, I guess."

"Don't worry, honey. I'll make it exciting."

"I sure hope so."

She motioned for him to come closer. "Let's check you out so we can get this show on the road."

"I need to use the head real quick," Jack said.

She pointed to the bathroom. "Don't leave it all in there. I like to earn my money."

In the bathroom, Jack took the gun from his waistband and put it in his coat pocket. Desiree was good-looking in an everyday sort of way, but the last thing he wanted to do was to have to pay for sex. Good sex, like the kind he and Kristy used to have in the beginning, was such an honest coupling that it made his chest ache with a hollowness he wished he'd never been forced to discover.

He'd heard that the rooms at the Ranch had video cameras hidden in them, but he didn't believe it. He was pretty sure he could refuse payment and still get what he came for and be down the road before the Ranch knew what hit it. He squeezed out a piss and walked out of the bathroom with the gun inside

86

his balled-up jacket. He unzipped his pants and she put a warm towel under his balls and checked him for the clap.

"Clean bill of health?" he said.

"A fine looking penis, Jack," she said. "We're going to have fun with it."

He set his jacket on the chair in the corner and laughed at himself for thinking he ever would have used the gun.

"What's the joke?" she asked.

"Nothing," he said, shaking his head. "Where were we?"

"Sixty for a half and half. That sound fair to you, Jack?" she said.

He stood in front of her, pants at his ankles, wondering if she'd leave with him. Just walk out right now. He had enough money to get them to Las Vegas or wherever a true redhead might want to go.

"Do you still want to do it?" she asked.

"Does anyone love you?" he asked her.

"You will after I'm through with you, honey," she said.

"I hope so," he said. "I'd really like to love you."

"Fork over sixty and you can start," she said.

"That sounds like a bargain," Jack said.

THE POTTERY

He could never decide which gun to take. If there was a lot of pipe to break up, the .410 and .22 rifles might not have enough pop. He'd been shooting the .30-30 since he was eight, but it had iron sights and in the middle of the night his eyes weren't what they used to be. He lifted the .270 Weatherby from its cushioned rest. Of all the pistols, rifles, and shotguns in the case, it was the only one Danny Padilla had bought himself, the only one that hadn't been fired by his father, re-sighted by a cousin, or handed down from an uncle. Just feeling its weight in his palm reassured him that this gun would always be enough.

He drove the two blocks from his house to the Pottery with his lights off just because he could. At two a.m. in Stanton the cops didn't bother wasting gas patrolling. When Manuel Diaz had called to tell him that a pipe had fallen over inside the Lincoln kiln, Danny thought the ringing of the phone was his alarm going off, and for an instant was relieved that it wasn't yet time to go to work.

He drove through the open gate of the plant, under a sign that read Franklin-Martin. The sign was suspended by two wires over the gate, and when the wind blew it swung wildly over the workers as they entered and exited the plant, seemingly ready to come down upon them like a guillotine at any moment. The Lincoln kiln was at the back of the plant, past sewer pipe stacked in the shape of pyramids and terra cotta ready to be sent to Oklahoma, shipping numbers written in chalk on the sides of the crates. It was early spring and the night air still carried winter's sting, but by the Lincoln kiln the men worked in T-shirts with jugs of cold water close by.

"*Mira*," Manuel said, removing two bricks next to the metal door at the back end of the kiln. Danny leaned in and looked. It took three days to turn clay into something useful. Every eight hours a forklift pushed flatbed cars full of roof tile, sewer pipe, and brick along railroad tracks through the kilns. In the middle of the kiln the temperature reached twenty-six-hundred degrees, the heat from the gas jets an unforgiving test of the clay.

At end of the kiln where the pipe and roof tile were stored to cool for a day, it was still about two hundred degrees. Danny pressed his cheek against the warmth of the brick and wished he was home asleep.

"Fourth car in," Manuel said.

Danny stretched his eyes open wide, focused, and found the rogue pipe leaning against the wall. There was only one, but it was enough to send all the pipe on the other cars toppling over if they continued to be pushed through. Because of the cost, kilns were only shut down as a last resort, so it was up to Danny to break up the pipe and allow the cars to continue through unimpeded. Danny's first summer at the Pottery one of the pipe setters returned from lunch full of three Bud talls, and two days later every car he had set collapsed upon each other smack in the middle of the Cordova kiln. After shutting down the kiln and letting it cool for a day, he and seven other young Mexicans were sent in to clean up the mess. In teams of two they climbed into asbestos suits, sprinted in and threw as much half-baked clay into a hopper as they could before their lungs began to ache and the skin on their foreheads felt like paper crinkling up moments before bursting into flame. They would peel off their suits outside the kiln, hand them to the next team, then stand in front of a fan sucking down water as fast as it was leaving their bodies and wait for their next turns.

Danny stepped back, loaded a bullet into the chamber of the rifle and pushed the bolt closed. He moved slowly because he shot better when the process was orderly, made him more aware that where this bullet went was all up to him. His first shot tore through a pipe twenty feet beyond the one he was trying to hit. His second ricocheted off the brick wall, and the third kicked up sparks as it hit the tracks.

"Should I call Leo?" Manuel asked.

"No, you shouldn't call Leo," Danny answered. When he turned to grab more bullets he saw that Manuel was grinning.

"That *panzón*," Danny said, "couldn't hit his ass with both hands if he fell on them."

Manuel laughed. "But he doesn't complain when we wake him up in the middle of the night."

"You've seen his wife. I'd be wanting to get out of bed, too," Danny said.

He shoved another bullet into the chamber, reminding himself to slow down, relax, breathe deep, and knock the fucking pipe down so he could go home. He adjusted his stance, kicking his left leg out. He had one leg a half-inch longer than the other so looking off balance was the only time he was ever in balance. His shot boomed through the kiln, and while it was still echoing in his ears Danny looked through the scope of his rifle and saw clay dust where the pipe used to be. He turned to Manuel and winked.

Manuel clapped his hands. "Now that's more like it. Good shooting, *compa.*"

"There's still a small piece hanging off the car," Danny said.

"Ah, *no problema*," Manuel said. "As long as it's not hitting the wall."

Danny was wide awake now. He felt he could hit anything. Even more, he wanted to. He poked the barrel of the rifle through the bricks and sighted in on the remaining piece of pipe. It was so small he could barely make it out, and even though he only had about six inches to work with between the wall and the car, the pipe was a memory with the first shot.

"Make sure you tell Leo about that one," Danny said, shaking his shoulder where the .270 had delivered its recoil.

Less than four hours later Danny was sitting with Skip Hutchins in the personnel office, which also doubled as the nurse's station. They had been having a cup of coffee every morning at 5:50 since getting promoted from yellow hats to white hats four years ago. Danny was recounting the story of the shooting when the plant manager, Frank Hollins, walked in. He'd been their first foreman when they had started at the Pottery straight out of high school almost twenty years ago.

Hollins had been one of the original take-no-shit guys, wrapping himself so tightly around his job that there was no room for anyone—co-worker or superior—to make him believe that there was a better way to do the job than the way he was doing it.

"You had to come in and shoot out the Lincoln last night?" Frank asked, pouring himself a cup of coffee.

"That's two kills already this year," Skip said. "One more and our boy gets sniper status."

"I guess no one bothers to tell me shit anymore," Frank said.

"Figured you had enough on your mind with the Oklahoma job," Danny said. "Besides, it was just one pipe."

"Who set it?" Frank asked.

"I'd have to go over the production tables."

"Well, tell me when you find out."

"It was a minor mistake," Skip said from his desk. "Happens all the time."

"Exactly," Frank said.

Skip looked out the window. Hollins had threatened to fire him a dozen years ago when Skip was a forklift driver and had dumped a pallet of terra cotta coming out of the fitting shed. Skip's been afraid of him ever since.

Danny jumped into the silence. "I don't know what good it'll do bitching someone out for not being perfect."

"But if I don't push them to be perfect," Frank said, "how will they ever get to be good?"

Danny shrugged.

"That Oklahoma job's looking nice," Skip said.

"Sure is. We should be shipping in two weeks. It's going to be one helluva good-looking building, I tell you," Frank said. "And between the three of us, it came along just in time. No one buys terra cotta anymore. Too expensive and a pain in the ass to install. We were damn close to shit-canning the whole department."

He put down his mug and walked to the door. "Damn, Skip. I never would've promoted you if I knew you made such bad coffee."

94

Danny poured himself another half cup and took his high blood pressure medication. "I think ol' Frank's been a boss too long," he said. "He's starting to sound like an asshole full time now."

"Yep. He actually believes he can be in charge of people," Skip said.

They sat without speaking, staring out into the yard. Clay particles floated in the slice of sun that dove between the smokestacks of the plant. The 5:55 whistle blew, but neither moved. The door to the office opened, pulling them from their thoughts.

"Not even six o'clock and already one of these geniuses injures himself," the nurse said as she entered. She wiped her shoes on the tile floor, a cream-colored glaze with brown swirling etchings in it, tile that the Pottery hadn't produced in fourteen years but was all over town in bathrooms, patios, and entryways.

"That's why you get paid the big bucks," Danny said.

Linda Nucchi, five foot ten and Sicilian dark, who insisted on waking at four fifteen every morning in order to do her hair and makeup, walked over and gave Skip a kiss on the cheek, and Danny, as Skip sat with his back to them, a kiss on the lips. "How are my two favorite men in Stanton?" she said.

"What happened?" Skip asked.

"Jamie Gonzalez cut his arm on a broken piece of pipe."

"Stitches?" Skip asked, pulling a form from his desk drawer.

"Nah. I cleaned and dressed it and told him to walk with his eyes open from now on."

Linda put her purse on her desk. "I just noticed something," she said, pointing to Danny. "You look like hell."

"I had to come shoot out the Lincoln last night. This morning, I mean."

"You are my hero," she said, sitting down, her long legs sliding out from her skirt. "If you weren't married, I'd date you."

For six months now Danny and Linda had been sleeping to-gether. No one knew, not her husband, his wife, or anyone at the plant, even Skip. It was a secret that had to be cultivated in such a small town, a small plant, but Linda delighted in testing the bounds of common sense, and that turned Danny on all the more.

The six o'clock whistle screamed and Danny automatically went for the door, stopping to pour another cup of coffee. "Christ, I hate to do this, but I just can't stay awake. I'll be pissing like a race horse all day," he said.

"There's a lady present," Linda said.

"Yeah, but Skip's used to my language," Danny said.

He walked across the open yard toward his office. Every-thing intensified the moment he stepped from the light of the yard to the shadows of the kiln area. Dozens of workers were already in constant motion, trying to keep time with each other. The forklift drivers had just dropped off pallets of clay rings that the pipe would be set on. The setters were laying them out and would finish just as the forklifts returned with sixteen- and twenty-inch sewer pipe. More forklifts would arrive as the set-ters were halfway done with each car. The driver would climb onto a pallet suspended six feet in the air by the forks of the Hyster and begin stuffing ten- and twelve-inch pipe inside the larger pipe.

After making sure his crew was present and working, Danny walked to the main factory, then to clay prep, and fi-nally to speed seal, where he conferred with the other white hats about the production schedule. His temples burned from all the caffeine he'd had, and he stopped to pee twice before making it back.

He shut the door to his office, but it was not made for pri-vacy—either for him or the workers. Horns beeped at almost set intervals as forklifts came and went and came back again. The staccato bursts of the handheld pneumatic lifts the setters used to grab and move pipe blended together into an abrupt, powerful chorus that his closed door was no match for.

96

Danny took off his boots and socks and rubbed his feet. They were a mess. He'd had surgery to remove bone spurs in his heels two years ago and the doctor said it'd be a miracle if they didn't come back. Athlete's foot was everywhere. He pulled baby powder from a desk drawer and threw it onto his feet. It's these damn steel toe boots, he thought.

He opened the logbook and began tracing when the cars from last night had been set. There were so many things that could go wrong in turning clay to pipe—the rings the pipe sit on could be dry and cracked, the calibration of the machine that cut the pipe could be off. A hair too thick or thin would be all it would take to make the pipe wobbly as it was moved through the kiln. The mixture of the clay could be uneven, leaving the pipe with no integrity to withstand the firing process. Too many things to take into account before settling on the care-lessness of one of his workers, Danny thought. So it didn't sur-prise him that that was the first thing Frank Hollins considered.

At lunchtime Danny was halfway across the yard to the per-sonnel office when Hollins caught up to him.

"I checked the log," Danny said. "Those cars were set three days ago on swing shift by either Morales, Ruiz, Vasquez, or Gomez. It's impossible to tell who."

"I ain't got time to chew out four people. You tell Manuel to come see me. He needs to learn to crack the whip a little more anyway."

Danny didn't answer.

"I've actually got something more important to run by you," Frank said. He was short with wide shoulders that made him seem taller than he actually was, plus he tended to stand close to people so they didn't realize how short he really was.

Danny put his fingers to his eyes, feeling the puffiness un-der them, sensing the black rings from the lack of sleep. "Shoot," he said, closing his eyes to Frank's presence.

"How do you feel about taking a trip to Oklahoma?"

"You mean for the terra cotta job?"

"You know how important this contract is. It's the biggest thing we've done in a decade and corporate wants someone there to represent us and to be a consultant to the construction team."

"Vic's in charge of terra cotta," Danny said, opening his eyes.

"Oh, hell, can you imagine? He hasn't been fifty miles from Stanton his whole life. I can just see him spitting tobacco juice on the architect's shoes." Frank laughed, then said, "You started out in the fitting shed. It'll be no problem."

"What about Henry? Isn't that what assistant managers are for?"

"Ol' Henry is getting a little long in the tooth. Might even retire in a year or two, I hear. Plus, he doesn't even own a tie."

"How long are we talking about?"

"Two weeks. A month tops."

"I was supposed to be on vacation at the end of the month," Danny said. "Going to take the kids camping." And with plans to meet Linda at her house for lunch the other days, he thought to himself.

Frank shrugged. "It's up to you. I know we'd all appreciate it."

"I'll think about."

"I knew you would." Danny wanted to tell him to go to hell for saying that, but knew it was true so what would be the point.

Inside the personnel office Linda pressed her entire body against him as soon as Skip went to the bathroom. She was an inch taller than him, and he had to push back hard in order not to be moved backwards. He shoved his hands into her dark hair, losing his fingers in its thickness. Their first night to-gether, after Bull Jorgensons's retirement party, Danny had a list of excuses ready to convince her to sleep with him: married young to a woman he might not even have married if she hadn't gotten pregnant, the boredom of living in the same small town his whole life, the prospect of working at the Pottery for the rest of it. Linda looked at him and said, "So you think that makes you special?" and they hadn't talked about what they were doing since.

Danny grabbed her ass with both hands, taking handfuls of skirt with him. "I can't wait to fuck you again," he said.

"Then do me right here," she said.

He thrust against her. "Bring it on, *sancha*," he said, but just then the toilet flushed and he backed away from her.

She grabbed him by the crotch and unzipped his pants. "I'm serious," she said.

Skip came out of the bathroom, head down, washing his hands.

Danny turned away, coughed and zipped up his pants. "Next time," he said.

"If you say so," Linda said.

As always, Manuel came in twenty minutes early, just as Danny was finishing compiling the production numbers for his shift. Danny asked him once why he gave the company so much extra time. "Think about it," he had told Manuel, "twenty minutes every day over a whole year is about two weeks worth of work."

"Ah, you know," Manuel responded with his big smile and crooked teeth, "I like to get settled, see everyone, make sure everything's all right."

But Danny could tell by the way Manuel didn't look at him that he was like all the other immigrants and *pochos* at the Pottery, so grateful not to be dodging bullets in Juarez or picking cotton in Bakersfield that they'd gladly spend an extra twenty minutes a day pulling clay from fire. He wanted to ask Manuel what all that hard work had gotten him. He still had the yellow hat of a lead man, not the white hat of a foreman, but Danny didn't want to insult his friend.

Danny was a *pocho* like Manuel but his parents had come to Stanton as school children so Danny was thought of by most of the workers at the Pottery as being more Stanton than Mexican.

He had the last name and dark skin but didn't know much of the language beyond what he had learned at the plant. His parents had spoken Spanish only when they didn't want Danny and his sisters to know what they were talking about. He wasn't blind to the fact that he was the only white hat with brown skin, or that when he had been promoted it was probably because he wasn't thought of in the same way as the half dozen Mexicans who had more seniority than him. In Stanton, Danny figured, you had to get what you could when you could get it. He would not be fooled. That would be his victory.

He called Manuel into the office. "I wanted to give you a heads up," he said. "Hollins wants to chew on some of your ass."

"*Por que?*"

"That car last night was set on your shift."

"I can't check every piece that goes in the kiln."

"I know, I know. You're preaching to the choir, *compa,*" Danny said.

Manuel took off his baseball cap and put on his yellow hard hat, smoothing his thinning hair on the sides of his head. "Why does he like to yell so much?"

"*Porque se puede,*" Danny said.

Manuel nodded.

Danny's wife and daughter and son were gone when he came home from work. His youngest, Bobby, had a Little League game. They left a note for him to meet them at the game.

He showered, rinsed the tub of the dirt that had fallen from his body, and lay down on the bed. His back was sore from all the walking he'd done during the week. The hard pan that was the Pottery floor was as unforgiving as cement, besides being uneven and full of ruts—the exact worst combination for a man with one leg longer than the other. He wished his daughter was there to walk on his back. Kristen was sixteen and just over one hundred pounds so he didn't know how much longer he'd be

100

able to handle her on his back, or what he'd do when he couldn't. He closed his eyes. Oklahoma. A month in a place that's as dusty as clay prep, dealing with architects and contractors who didn't need his help, then coming back to a bitter Vic Sanders in the fitting shed. Fuck me. But his kids were as smart as coyotes and were talking as if college were in their future, and Danny was determined to let that be an option for them. Promotions were somewhat arbitrary at the Pottery, but Hollins wouldn't be able to ignore his going to Oklahoma.

Two hours later, Danny woke in the same position he'd lain down in. "Oh, shit," he said when he rolled over and saw what time it was.

He didn't see his wife's car at the park. As he drove uptown toward the pizza parlor where they normally went after games, Danny passed the Oasis and saw a dozen cars belonging to workers from the Pottery, including Skip and Linda's.

"Well, if it ain't Mr. Corporate Representative," Wally Burgess from maintenance said when he walked in.

Danny nodded and smiled. "What can I say? I clean up a little better than you slobs."

Kenny Stevens from speed seal handed him a whiskey and coke. "Oklahoma, huh? Too bad we weren't doing a job in Hawaii or someplace like that."

"No shit," Danny said and took a drink.

"Something tells me," Skip said from the corner of the bar, "that if we were doing a job in Hawaii, Frank Hollins would be getting on that plane, not you."

"Here, here," Linda said and raised her glass.

Danny and the others raised their glasses to hers. "What will we do," she continued, "without our sharpshooter for a whole month? We may as well shut down the whole plant."

Linda was at a table back from the bar, eating dinner with her husband. She was five years older than Danny, her husband a dozen years older than her. At times Danny wondered if they would end up together ten, fifteen years from now. This was one of those times. He took a healthy sip of his drink and pushed the thought out of his mind. The whiskey eased its way down his back to his legs, somehow knowing just what to loosen and what to numb.

Skip slapped him on the back. "Big week for you, *amigo*."

Danny tapped his glass against Skip's beer bottle. "Yep. Thank God it's over."

He ordered another drink while Skip, Linda, and the others rehashed the events of the past week at work. Danny could stay here all night with these people, but not if all they had inside them was the Pottery. He left without finishing his drink.

He turned the corner to his house, saw his wife's car and wondered how upset she'd be. She would be sitting on the couch and would click the volume on the television up every time he tried to talk to her. He made a U-turn in the middle of the street and drove to the Pottery.

He wished he hadn't stopped with Linda earlier, that he had told Hollins no about going to Oklahoma, but his body would not do the bidding of his heart, nor would his mouth do the bidding of his brain. They both somehow knew that he was not ready for what would come afterwards, that frustrations were manageable but repercussions were devastating in their possibilities.

A dozen cars sat outside the dented doors of the Cordova kiln, row after row of moist, shiny clay waiting to be transformed into roof tile. The Cordova wouldn't run a swing shift until the summer when construction picked up. When they were first married, Danny and his wife would take walks around town after dinner and he would point out the terra cotta on the buildings, the brick and roof tile on the houses. He could tell she didn't care that much. No one who didn't work at the plant did, really. To them brick and tile was something to be bought and used—it wasn't anything that anyone had made.

Danny walked around the kiln. Its gas jets, undetectable during the rush of the workday, blew with what seemed like the force of a turbine jet. Forklifts were scattered around the area like a child's toys at the end of the day. An occasional shout from the Lincoln kiln traveled through the empty building. Danny pushed his fingers through one of the tiles. The clay was cool and his entire hand tingled. He couldn't remember the last time he had actually touched a tile at this stage of production. He knocked one onto the ground. He turned one of the bottom tile on the front car a hair inward and caved in one side with his thumb. It would be imperceptible to the driver pushing in the cars, but the tile would never hold up to the jostling of being moved through the kiln.

Danny drove home to wait for the call. It might not come until tomorrow night, or the night after, but it would come, he was sure of that.

EAT THE WORM

When the causeway was flooded, water stretched across it seemingly without bounds. Designed to keep the surrounding farms from flooding by taking what wasn't needed, there were no levees to corral the type of storms that had already come during the year. The water was free to roam as far as it wanted seeking its own level.

The causeway permanently separated Stanton from Sacramento, and as Todd crossed it, he thought how rare that it was flooded this early in the fall, and how a few simple days of sunshine would take it all away.

The drive from the Bay Area took two and a half hours, but as they exited the expressway and dropped down onto Highway 65 and eventually into Stanton, Todd wished it were longer.

"We can live in your hometown," his wife had said when she told him about the job offer in Sacramento. "A third generation of Randles. A whole new tradition."

"My hometown," Todd told her, "is interested only in the past, either reliving it or lying about how good it was."

That first night, after unpacking, Todd went downtown to pick up a pizza. He passed the Franklin-Martin plant where his dad worked, and a block later the Oasis, where his dad drank, and not always in that order. The plant was filled with clay sewer pipe, brick, and roof tile, and surrounded by a chain-link fence with circular razors on top. The joke around town was that the fence wasn't to keep thieves out, but to keep the workers in. He crossed the railroad tracks to the side of town where his dad lived.

His dad's house was dark except for the ground lights standing like sentries among his roses. The lawn was as smooth and trim as a putting green—no one ever cut across it when they visited. Birch trees, planted when Todd was ten, towered over the yard like giant pillars, casting shade halfway across the street during the summer.

It was a minor miracle, the way his yard looked. The ground in Stanton was choked with clay, which was great for making the pipe and brick at the Pottery, but terrible for everything else.

That soil, paired with summer days over a hundred degrees, made most yards unable to sustain little more than a mulberry tree, whose branches had to be cut back to a naked nub every year, or thick, twisted juniper bushes that were impossible to shape into anything anyone wanted to look at. And even if you did manage to get something to keep, the soil rejected all roots, sending them back to the surface regardless of what was in their way: sidewalks, driveways, sprinkler systems.

"Town still look the same?" Kelly asked as they sat cross-legged on their bed, eating.

"Only more so," Todd answered. He set the pizza box down and crawled up on her.

"Where do you think you're going, mister?" she said.

"I figured I'd let you experience the joy that is my penis inside you."

"How about if you just lay with me," she said.

"I'm no doctor," Todd said, "but I'm pretty sure a baby's not going to make itself."

"You're a day late and a dollar short, my love. I started my period today."

"Shit. I'm sorry."

"Don't sweat it. If at first you don't succeed, try, try, again. Besides, it's not your fault."

"Yeah, but I don't want people thinking I can't do my job. I have a reputation in this town, you know," Todd said, smiling.

"And I'm sure I'll find out what it is in no time," Kelly said.

Todd had an interview the next day with Louie Mazzoni, an old friend of his dad's who owned a small property management firm in town. Louie had come over from Pieve San Paolo, Italy, thirty years earlier, and his accent had somehow not only survived, but was as strong as the day he'd stepped foot in California.

"I appreciate the time, Louie," Todd said as he took a seat across the desk from him.

"When your old man told me you were moving back I said, get that sonofabitch in here, I'll find something for him to do," he said, leaning his chair back against the wall.

"Seems like you've got everything under control here. Please don't feel obligated," Todd said.

"Don't you worry about that," Louie said. "I like your old man a lot, but not enough to go broke for him."

They laughed.

"How is that sonofabitch doing?" Louie asked. "I haven't seen him since he cheated me in lowball at the Oasis."

Todd shifted in his chair. "I actually haven't seen him yet. Been busy unpacking and stuff."

"*Madone.* You gotta get over there. Today. No screwing around." Todd nodded.

"He sure is happy to have you back. Every time I see him, he tells me, 'Todd is moving back.' I know, I know, I tell him. I tell him I'm already sick of you before you even show up."

Todd laughed.

"I tell you what, Todd, I've been wanting to go after some business in Nicolaus, Loomis, Yuba City. Now that Sacramento is growing so much, those *pezzonovante* property managers over there don't want to be bothered with these little towns. I need someone to help research which complexes to go after, create a little presentation kit, do the bidding."

"Sounds like a good plan, but I have no experience doing any of that, Louie," Todd said, relieved he wouldn't have to take a job his dad had surely set in motion for him.

"No, but you got a college education. And you've been living in Frisco. You've been around. After we get some new contracts you can manage them. I tell you, I work in the sewers in Luca when I am a boy, go in the Army for a few years, get yelled at all day. This is the easiest money I've ever made."

"How can I refuse an offer like that?" Todd said.

"You can't, you sonofabitch," Louie said, coming around the desk to hug Todd. "You go home, have a nice dinner with your wife and start the day after tomorrow."

Todd nodded.

"Your wife, she still have the big knockers?" Louie asked.

Todd smiled. "Pretty big, yeah."

Louie shook his head. "It must take you all day to climb up there."

"And sometimes all night," Todd said.

It was raining when Todd left. He went home and began unpacking the boxes they hadn't gotten around to last night. The rain continued, growing harder as morning stretched into afternoon. He decided to go downtown and see who he could see, stopping at the Oasis before he even got to the state highway that ran through the center of town. He parked in the lot behind the bar so his dad wouldn't see his car on the way home from work.

"Well, looky what the cat drug in," Jack Dixon, a friend from high school, boomed when Todd walked in. "Decided to grace us with your presence, did you, college boy?"

"How could I stay away from your sense of humor?" Todd said, sitting down at his table.

The Oasis was all wood: oak hardwood floors, redwood paneling on the walls, thick mahogany picnic-style tables. The years had stripped away the bar's shine and countless spilled beers had soaked to its core, leaving the wood permanently wet looking.

"Heard you moved back," Jack said, pushing a beer over to him. "Gonna work with Louie, huh?"

"Seems like it," Todd said, not at all surprised that his business was public knowledge before he had even moved back.

"Well, you know one thing. It won't be boring."

"Speaking of work, shouldn't you be out doing some of it right now?"

"Paint won't dry in the rain. Didn't they teach you that in college?"

"I must have been absent that day," Todd said.

They sat and watched ESPN as workers from the plant trickled in, stomping their wet feet on the floor and snapping

110

the rain from their jackets before draping them over chairs. The clay dust on their arms had turned to mud in the rain and they took turns wiping themselves down with a rag from the bar.

Todd got up to get a pitcher of beer. A hand reached out from a stool and pinched his ass. "How long are you going to sit over there and ignore me?" It was Pam Jenkins, the younger sister of a classmate.

"You're just so damn good-looking I've got to get a few drinks in me to work up the courage to say hello," Todd said.

"Still as full of shit as ever, I see," she said, reaching up and kissing him on the cheek. "Heard you were coming back home."

"Can I buy you a drink?" Todd asked.

"I'll buy you one," Pam said. "A welcome back present." She signaled for two kamikazes.

"What are you doing now?" he asked. "Married, kids?"

"Working at the plant, where else? Keeping the books. And no and no."

Todd made a point of looking her up and down. "I didn't think that body had busted out any kids."

"Give it up," she said, "I'm not sleeping with you."

"How about a reach around then? That's the kind of welcome back gift I'd really like."

They laughed and threw down their shots.

"How 'bout your brother? It's been at least five years since I've seen his ugly mug," Todd said.

"He's still in the service. Stationed down in San Diego. He's a big-time Jehovah's Witness now. Fucking nut."

Jack yelled that he was getting thirsty. Todd delivered the pitcher to his table and stepped into the hallway that lead to the restrooms to call Kelly on his cell phone.

"I was just getting ready to call you. I won't be home for dinner."

"O.T. on the first day?" he said.

"You know how it is," she said. "How'd your interview go?"

"It was a ball-buster, but the job's mine if I want it."

111

"We're in the money, now," she yelled into the phone.

"When are you planning on being home?"

"I'll be here at least another hour, then the publisher wants to take me out to dinner to meet some advertisers. I'm looking at about nine or later."

Kelly was the new managing editor of a lifestyle magazine in Sacramento. The money was about the same as the job she had in San Francisco where she was an assistant editor.

"You'll miss all the concerts and Golden Gate Park and the Zam Zam Club," he said when she told him about the Sacramento offer.

She squeezed his hand and said, "Managing editor."

He went back to Pam. "Do you see my old man much at work?"

"Besides every day? He says you're going to own this town in no time."

"And we all know how much he likes to exaggerate," Todd said.

"Yeah. How many touchdowns did he score in that homecoming game against Ponderosa? Four?"

"I think it's up to five now."

Pam laughed. Todd bought another round of kamikazes.

"Does he come in here much?" Todd asked.

"He was here Saturday night with a muscle shirt on, bird dogging old lady Flowers all night long. He used to come in on Sundays but now that it's football season he stays home and watches the games by himself, I guess."

Todd and Pam took their drinks and joined Jack at the table. They swapped old stories about growing up in Stanton, then Jack and Pam turned to Todd with questions about going away to college and living in San Francisco, questions littered with misconceptions, awe, and contempt. Todd didn't mind. He used to ask the same questions of his cousin David when he came home from UCLA on Christmas break. At fourteen, insight into the world that lay beyond the causeway seemed to Todd the greatest thing a person could possess.

112

Another round of drinks and it was dark. Todd couldn't remember the last time he had spent all afternoon drinking like this, but there was something undeniably comforting about walking into a place and knowing people, about not having to explain who you were because, for better or worse, they already knew.

"Time for me to scramble," he said.

"Wait up, I'm heading out, too," Pam said and chugged her beer.

They walked through the parking lot to her car. "Are you glad to be back?" she asked.

"Had a helluva good time tonight," Todd said.

"Well, it's good to have you back," she said, extending her arms for a hug.

"Thanks," he said, stepping into her embrace, putting his cheek next to hers. She had full, wavy hair, and it lay lightly in his hand. Their heads moved in rhythm off each other's shoulder and Todd knew what was coming next but didn't stop. They kissed. Then kissed again, gripping each other tight.

Todd pulled away and looked around the parking lot but no one else was around. "I'm supposed to be married," he said.

"That's okay," Pam said. "She's not a Stanton girl." She grabbed his crotch. "And remember, you'll always be a Stanton boy."

They kissed again. "I'm here every Friday night," she said. Todd pulled away and walked off to his car without saying a word or looking back at her.

He drove through town out to the frontage road that ran next to the causeway. It was the same road he and all his friends had cruised and drank and screwed on as teenagers, the same road his dad drove on twenty years before them, the same road his child would drive on twenty years after if he stayed in Stanton. The road was dirt, but packed hard by use, and was exactly at the point where the town's jurisdiction ended and the county's began, so neither bothered sending out a car to patrol it. It was the perfect road to do nothing on.

113

"Jesus Christ," Todd said. "Jesus Christ." He took a deep breath and slapped the steering wheel. Not even two days and already he resented the closeness of the town, the smallness of it in his skin like a rash.

He stopped to piss. The rain had quit and the causeway shined black from the light of the moon. It looked like a never-ending sea. In the distance, planes started their descent to the Sacramento airport. The causeway didn't immediately separate Stanton from Sacramento, but it stood as a reminder that no matter what happened in the future, no matter how much Sacramento grew, Stanton would never get swallowed up by it, could never truly be a part of it, even it if wanted to be. Though the entire Sacramento Valley was flat, Sacramento was still too far away to be seen. Todd remembered his first trip into Sacramento as a boy, how the high-rises appeared suddenly after miles of fields, and the traffic and noise and activity made it seem that there was something fertile in the city that Stanton inherently lacked.

He drove back through downtown. It was empty, the hardware and grocery stores dark and hollow. The almost bankrupt feed store had converted part of its space to a coffee shop. *Mocha and Alfalfa* the sign read. The building boom that was sending Sacramento sprawling in all directions had so far avoided Stanton, and Todd gathered that the town was happy about that fact. The town's three stoplights blinked in time. In high school, coming home late from a party, he would drive through the middle of town before heading home, comforted that the next day and every one that followed would be exactly the same.

He parked across the street from his dad's house. After becoming certified as a dental hygienist, Todd's mother left his dad and Stanton for Colorado to live with her sister, and within a year was married to the dentist she had gone to work for. Todd was five. She sent a letter his senior year in high school offering to pay for his college. When he showed it to his dad, thinking he'd be relieved to have some of the burden off him,

114

he ripped it up and punched at the pieces of paper as they floated in the air around him and called her a bitch and a whore for five unending minutes. His dad worked holidays and every other weekend while Todd went through college, and when Todd graduated, said, "Now make sure you do better than your old man."

He imagined Kelly leaving him. If she found about Pam she might because she was the type of person who was more concerned with getting on to new opportunities than fixing problems. Todd always suspected he had this laziness in him, a willingness to settle for the first thing he found comfort in. Maybe not a laziness, but certainly a lack of ambition. Growing up, everyone he knew worked at the Pottery. Everyone made the same amount of money and had the same size house, so he came to believe that the worth of a person was measured in other ways. Would you keep a friend from getting his ass kicked even if he deserved it, would you help your cousin roof his house without knowing anything about construction, how well could you hold your liquor? Those where the questions he asked himself.

One of the reasons he fell in love with Kelly was because of how confident she was of what she wanted, the way she could be so single-minded, so uninterruptible. He had no doubt that she would eventually be promoted to editor-in-chief at the magazine, or that when they had kids she would be their room parent when they started school and in charge of the snack bar at little league games. As a teenager he never had a burning desire to leave Stanton but always assumed, in a vague sort of way, that he would, that he would go away to college like his cousin David because he was smart. But unlike his cousin, Todd assumed he would eventually come back and be able to move seamlessly between Stanton and the rest of the world.

Chico State was only seventy-five miles from Stanton, but for Todd it was a different world, a much bigger world. Though at the northern end of the Sacramento Valley and flat like Stanton, mountains could be seen from anywhere in town. He and Kelly would drive up to Forest Ranch—only twenty-five miles from Chico but a two thousand foot climb in elevation—and hike all day, or drive forty more miles to Chester when the first snow of the season hit the mountains. Suddenly, life outside of Stanton seemed to be his only choice, that going back would be infinitely more difficult than leaving ever had been.

He and Kelly were both twenty-eight and had been married only two years. Their lives weren't completely set—options were still theirs to consider. Work or travel, children or no children, together or apart—none of that had been permanently answered yet, at least in Todd's mind.

Kelly was in bed reading when he got home. "Where have you been?" she asked.

"Hooked up with some old buddies at the Oasis."

"Good for you." She smiled, her full cheeks rising, almost pushing her eyes shut. Her face was short, though her short blonde hair made it seem longer than it was. "Tell me about your job."

Todd lay close to her, putting both hands around her neck and kissing her.

"Enough about business, how about some pleasure?" he said. He held her tight, wanting more than anything to slip inside her and wipe away the past few hours.

"Tomorrow night. I've got to get up early, and you're home late," she said.

Todd continued holding her.

"That reminds me," she went on. "Meet me in Sacramento for dinner tomorrow. The publisher is taking the staff and spouses out to dinner."

Todd gave up, sighing and letting his hands fall away from her body. "I don't want to take that job with Louie," he said. "I'm not going to take it."

"What are you talking about? It sounds like a great opportunity."

"Fuck it," he said, rolling away from her. "There are a lot of things I could do."

116

"What, are you going to work at the plant with your dad? Do they have a management trainee program I'm unaware of?"

"There's plenty of jobs in Sacramento. I don't have to settle for one in Stanton."

"Doesn't sound like you'd be settling for anything."

"We're okay financially. I can take my time and find something I'd really like to do. I have a college degree, damn it."

"I thought you wanted to have a kid," Kelly said. "That's going to take both of us working."

"I wouldn't mind being Mr. Mom while I look around."

"Well, I would."

"Of course you would." He went into the bathroom, brushed his teeth hard, and washed his face twice.

"What's wrong, Todd?" Kelly asked. "Are you not happy that we moved back?"

He shrugged.

"I can't help you unless you tell me what's wrong."

"Not everything can be met as a challenge, Kelly. Tenacity only helps if you know what you want."

"Come on, what's our motto, honey? No whining, right?"

"Mottos are important," Todd said.

"Are you going to talk to me or smart-off all night?"

He sat on the bed. "The job just doesn't feel right."

"How so?"

"Fuck, I don't know," Todd said. He exhaled loudly. "Let's forget about it. It's probably just the booze talking."

He lay down. "Nothing worse than a melancholy drunk," he said.

He called Kelly at work the next day. "Are we still on for tonight?"

"Of course. I can't wait for you to meet everybody. The Firehouse between seven and seven-thirty."

"I'll be there," Todd said and hung up. He loved her for not holding grudges. She said they were a waste of time but he suspected that she didn't want anyone thinking they had ever gotten to her enough to make her angry.

At five-thirty Todd drove over to his dad's. Having to meet Kelly in Sacramento would give him an excuse for not staying long. He entered the house without knocking.

"Well, hey, now," Todd's dad said, rocking himself up from where he sat deep in the couch. "Come on in, son. Glad you remembered where I lived."

"I heard there was free booze here," Todd said.

"Always."

He sat on the couch, a cooler of beer between him and his dad. Todd's dad had on a sleeveless Oakland Raiders sweatshirt, his arm wide and flat as it lay across the ice-chest. Thirty years ago he'd been a five foot eleven, one hundred and ninety-five pound fullback full of piss and vinegar. After high school he went to the junior college across the causeway, rushed for eight hundred and forty-nine yards and got Todd's mom pregnant. He quit playing ball, took a job driving forklift at the Pottery, got married, then four years later, divorced.

A special Thursday night edition of Monday Night Football was on the television. Todd's dad turned to him as the theme music cued up. "The key to this game is our corners. If we can shut down their wide receivers one-on-one that'll allow us to blitz the shit out of Manning, put that big-foreheaded fuck on his ass."

"You just hate him 'cause he's good," Todd said.

"Damn straight. A good quarterback makes all the difference. Like back in high school we had Aaron Mitchell's old man. Christ, what a leader. Then at Sierra we had that lame fuck Bobby Evans and didn't win shit."

"How's work?" Todd wanted to cut him off before he reminisced all the way back to his Pop Warner days, though it was good to hear him speak with such confidence and enthusiasm. Too bad he never had the time to coach. But Todd knew that soon, lubricated by the beer, his contentment would slide away to bitterness and jealousy. He'd rant about missed tackles and blocks, and complain about how fat the lineman were, and how no ballplayer was worth a million dollars a year.

118

"Work's work," his dad said, handing Todd one of the two beers he fished out of the ice chest.

"I know what you mean."

"You taking that job with Louie? That sonofabitch," he said in an Italian accent.

"I don't know. Probably."

"Good. Come home clean at the end of the day. You know, he worked two jobs for about ten years when he first came over. Lived with his uncle in some shit apartment in Sacramento. And you know what, he bought that same apartment complex last year. You can learn a lot from a guy like that."

Todd shrugged.

"Hear from your mother lately?"

"She sent me a postcard from Yellowstone in July. Her and Dean were on vacation."

Todd's dad grunted and took a long pull of his beer. "Wannabe yuppie fucks."

By half-time the ice chest was empty. If Todd left for Sacramento right now he could blame the traffic and get away with it, but he didn't move.

He found a bottle of mezcal in the cupboard above the refrigerator. He'd heard that if you ate the worm you would see a vision. He wanted to see so many things. To see if he was humble enough to understand what he truly needed in order to be happy, and if he had the balls to reach for whatever it was. But he couldn't separate these things in his mind, couldn't pick one desire out from another.

"Oh, sweet Jesus," Todd's dad said when he saw the bottle.

"Don't back out on me now, old man."

Todd set up a tray with shot glasses and sliced limes. They saluted each other and threw down their shots.

Midway through the third quarter, a Raider caught a five-yard slant in, spun away from the first defender, juked the second and third, and outran the last three.

"Woo, look at that!" Todd's dad yelped, hitting the ice chest with his fist, the veins like cable in his arms. "If I'd had that kind of speed I'd be a millionaire today."

He was oblivious to everything as the touchdown was replayed. Todd could see him imagining himself in the player's place. "Jesus, have another drink," he said.

They had three shots during the third quarter. Todd lost track of how many they had after that. Just one shot of mezcal stays with you—the charcoal smell, the burning taste—but little by little they were getting down to the worm.

"Don't you have to work tomorrow?" Todd's dad asked as he poured them another shot.

"Speaking of work, you know, you should've been a groundskeeper. Your yard is beautiful. I mean it, it's fucking beautiful." Todd heard his voice and knew he was shitty drunk.

"Thank you," his dad said and smiled wide. "It's no special talent, though. Just hard work."

"How come no one else's lawn looks as good as yours?"

"You just answered your own question, kid. Now, tell me what's happening in your life."

"We're thinking of having a kid, me and Kelly."

"That's terrific." His dad went to slap Todd's knee but missed.

"You think?"

"Sure. Kelly's a good athlete, right? Besides, you'll be a good father." He closed his eyes and drank his shot. His head bobbed from side to side. His face was flush, veins showing in his cheeks, all his boozing rising to the surface.

"You'll be a good father because you're a better man than me. I'd take more pride in that except I know you've tried to do everything in your life the opposite of me."

Todd threw back his shot and looked at his dad. His lips burned. "That's not true. None of it."

His dad pushed himself up from the couch and stumbled to the bathroom. The flush of the toilet was followed by heavy staggering footsteps down the hall to the bedroom. Todd grabbed the bottle and tipped it, the warm tequila filling his mouth, the worm slipping between his teeth and down his throat like a bitter promise.

He sat on the couch for fifteen minutes with the lights off but no vision came. And it didn't come as he dumped the ice from the cooler in the sink, or as he washed the shot glasses and threw away the used lime rinds. The only thing he was sure of was that if you stayed in Stanton, nothing was expected of you, but if you dare leave, everything was expected of you, like there was some kind of knowledge beyond the town's borders that you were supposed to gain. But for Todd, it felt like trying to hold water in his hands. You were supposed to be smarter, richer, more charismatic, know how the world worked. You were supposed to be better, and he felt none of those things.

He was almost out the door when his dad called for him. "Todd, Todd."

Todd walked slowly down the dark hallway, figuring his dad had fallen out of bed. It wouldn't have been the first time. Pushing open the door, Todd saw that his dad was in bed but naked, his whiteness shinning in the dark. He had an erection.

"Todd, go get your mother. Get your mother. Please. Go get your mother."

Todd snapped the door shut and started running down the hall then stopped and went back. His dad was passed out, his hard-on fading away. Todd pulled the covers tight around his shoulders and set his alarm, then filled a glass with water and set it next to the clock. Todd pressed his lips against his dad's forehead, holding them there for a long time until he thought the hot skin would sear his lips.

He called Kelly from the kitchen. He had betrayed his wife twice in two days, and there was a part of him that wished she were out doing something that would hurt him.

"You missed a good dinner," she said.

"I had to see my dad."

Silence.

"I'm coming home now."

"Don't do me any favors."

More silence.

"Is he all right? Your dad." Kelly asked.

"Depends on your definition of all right," Todd said.

"Well, do you think you're all right?"

"I'm really sorry about missing dinner. I guess this move's knocked me for a loop."

"Not good enough," Kelly said.

"I don't know what it is, Kelly. I mean, I had a great time growing up here. I was popular in high school and all that shit. But now I don't feel attached to anything."

"What about me?"

"I think that if I left tomorrow, you could be happy without me."

She sucked in her breath like he'd punched her. "That's a shitty thing to say."

"It's a shitty way to feel," Todd said.

"You should have more faith in me. In us," Kelly said.

"Will you wait up for me? Please, just wait up for me."

"Todd…"

"That's all I'm asking, just wait up for me. I'm trying to have more faith in myself, Kelly," he said.

"You'd better hurry."

"That's good enough," he said.

"You may not think so when you get here."

Todd drove with both hands steadying the wheel. He drove the length of town to get home and see his wife.

BUILDING

Found out yesterday that I'm going to be a father for the first time at the age of forty. That may be late compared to most of my friends but I'm about average for my family. My dad had me at thirty-six, my Uncle Rob had my cousin Jimmy at forty-four, and my grandfather busted out my Uncle Pete at fifty-three. Our rifles never run out of bullets, my dad likes to joke.

Melissa is only eight weeks along so we haven't told anyone yet. It's nice to have a secret, especially in a small town like Stanton. We've been married nine years so it isn't like starting a family has been our main concern, but I have to admit, having Mel pregnant has got me thinking.

I guess that's why I was on Highway 32 heading towards Chester early on a Saturday morning. It was dark when I left but as I climbed out of the Sacramento Valley toward the southern edge of Lassen Park, the sun had begun creeping over an un-named mountain in the distance, balancing on its peak before continuing its ascent. Until a few years ago me and my dad deer hunted up here, but he got too old and I became disinterested. I didn't grow tired of hunting really, but since none of my friends or relatives hunt, it just kinda faded away.

I'm not one who normally dwells on what was or what might have been. You spend too much time doing that and your past becomes your present. But like I said, having a kid had got me thinking about what kind of life my boy or girl will have growing up in Stanton. What memories will he have to pass down to his child when he's in my place thirty or forty years from now? I know that's all pretty basic stuff, probably every guy in my situation has pondered on the same things, but that's all right. It doesn't make what I'm going through any less significant. We're all only different at the margins, but those margins are everything.

It was two weeks before the opening day of deer season and I was set to begin building my new house any day. We probably couldn't even get tags this late, but still, I thought maybe the old man and I could at least come up for the first weekend.

I turned off the highway just before the bridge at Deer Creek and followed the logging road six miles into the mountainside. There was something mysterious about leaving the highway for this place, a place where signs gave way to landmarks and the petty noises of the world were swallowed by its silence.

Hunters have their own language up here. Ask someone how his hunt went and you might get an answer like, *I was hunting over by Slate Creek when a big sally and spike/fork came down the slide. He was small but I was gonna run him off with an arrow in him. I drew down on him, but he jumped the string and took off.*

Just by crossing over the highway onto the dirt road, I felt like a hunter again.

I drove to the upper road on the backside of the hill where we used to hunt. The main road was easy traveling, having been packed down by logging trucks, but the side roads were powdered with dust three inches thick. I drove with the windows up and when I stopped had to wait a full ten seconds for the trailing dust to pass. I walked into the woods and down to the lower road, across it into the gully and up to the top of the next hill. Even though it was two weeks before deer season and I was alone, I walked slowly and carefully, trying to minimize my presence.

I walked past our main stands: my dad's at the top of the first hill, mine, which used to be my Uncle Pete's, east of his and down towards the lower road. They had been built fifty years ago, two by sixes and large plywood platforms covering the expanse of two tall pines, a dozen spikes for climbing pounded into the trees. On the way back up the hill I checked out the stands we had put up the past decade, forced to look for new places to hunt because of too many hunters and too few deer. Despite how bad the hunting was those last few years, my dad, bound by habit and history, wouldn't give up the hillside so the new stands were simply farther and farther from our original trails.

I stopped under a cedar where I had put up a portable stand a few years back. A rusted chain was still wrapped around the tree and the holes where I had screwed in deer mees to climb up it had closed. Ever since the Nelson Pine Company bought this land they've tried to discourage hunters from building permanent stands, claiming the nails and spikes can be danger-ous to loggers if they hit them with their chainsaws. From the moment he saw the first sign against permanent stands my dad insisted that we use only portables, even though they're a pain in the ass to put up and take down, and are a third of the size of our permanent ones. But then, the old man and I have rarely agreed on what rules to follow. I'd build permanent stands all over this hillside if it were up to me, but would never steal from work like he used to.

He had been a foreman at the Pottery. Our house was a monument to clay-fired products: Spanish roof tile, brick exte-rior, kiln-fired tile in every room, pavers out on the patio. I could understand getting all that for our house, but he didn't stop there. Any third cousin by marriage or a friend of a friend could have a pallet of brick or tile bestowed upon them free of charge just for the asking. And in Stanton, where someone al-ways knew someone who knew my dad, the favors never stopped. I understand the power to make people feel good by giving them what they can't get themselves, but I always thought my dad went overboard, like he needed people to like him just a little too much.

Once a favor was asked, my dad would start bringing home brick or tile every day, the boxes hidden on the floorboard of the truck by a jacket or wedged behind the seat in the cab. Weekends were where he made the big hauls, going over to the plant early in the morning under the pretense of checking on his workers or a machine that had been acting up. He'd come home with boxes stacked just below the window of the camper shell on his truck.

None of the trails had many tracks on them, which was not much of a surprise. There weren't many locals in the area and it was too early for them to have started migrating. I drove over to the backside of Round Valley, on the edge of the game reserve. The only deer taken those last few years we hunted were taken over there.

I walked into the hillside and it was like a whole other world. Trails were chewed up with hoof prints, droppings were every ten steps, and a few trees even had scrapes on them. I followed the most traveled trail up the hill to where the trees gave way to rock, and shadows surrendered to the sun, and I knew that this was where the big bucks hung out.

I marked my path with reflective tape and committed to memory the exact spot where I went in, then drove over to the Bambi Inn for an early lunch. For years, hunters from Stanton had gone to the bar and the lore of the Bambi Inn had grown to mythic proportions. That no one went anymore only added to its legend.

I'd driven by it countless times throughout the years, but had never been inside. By the time I became old enough to legally drink, my dad and all his friends had stopped going, and with no one my age around, I was content to have a few beers around the campfire at night. But the same stories were trotted out every year, growing funnier, wilder, and more important with each telling.

I was eight the first time I came up here. My mom drove from Stanton to Forest Ranch, thirty miles east of Chico, on the Friday of the second weekend of the season to transfer me to my dad. Opening weekend was deemed too important to have him look after a child. They hunted all day, he said, and usually someone got one, which meant there would be hours of gutting and skinning, and I'd only get in the way. I didn't have my hunting license yet, but we would go fishing at Deer Creek on Saturday, then on Sunday we would drive home together.

That first year, as we turned toward Round Valley where everyone from Stanton camped, my dad turned to me and said, "Now, Eric, whatever goes on up here stays up here. I don't want you repeating anything you hear up here back in town. Understand?"

128

I nodded, not afraid at all of his serious tone, instead thrilled to be part of an adult life with all its mysteries and privileges. Of course, I couldn't keep my mouth shut, but was sure to tell the stories only to my friends, never to any adults. And when I told my friends about the way the men talked and drank, or who didn't come back to camp after a night at the bar, I relayed the information in a matter-of-fact tone, as if what went on in a deer camp was something a grown man took in stride. Most people in Stanton hunted something: quail, dove, turkey, pig, or deer, and my friends tried it like all kids in town were made to try it, but it never took with them. As an adult I wish some of them would hunt with me, but as a child it made me feel special to be the only one who hunted deer.

The Bambi Inn was old, small, and dark. About what I'd expected. I had no romantic notions that needed preserving or tearing down. I sat at the bar and waited for the bartender. There was a large four-pointer over the doorway that led to the dining room and a jack-a-lope over the old-time metal cash register.

The bartender came in through the back door, wiping his greasy hands on a rag. "Sorry about that," he said. "I was working on the snowplow, getting it ready for winter."

"No problem," I said. "I'll just have a beer."

"You up here scouting?" he asked as he set the beer in front of me.

I nodded.

"Where do you hunt?"

"Over by Round Valley, Slate Creek. That area."

"Lot of deer been taken out of there," he said.

"Not lately," I said, raising my mug to him in a salute. He looked to be in his mid-fifties, gray in his stubble, pockets of skin sagging beneath his eyes.

"Have you owned this place long?" I asked.

"'Bout ten years. But I've been bartending here for about thirty."

"Bet you've seen some wild nights in here."

"Let me tell you something," he said, wiping down the bar with the same rag he'd used on his hands. "Before I bought this place I worked at the casinos in Vegas. I'd work nine months there and spend the summers up here pouring drinks and fishing. I saw more crazy shit right here in this room than I ever saw on the Strip."

I smiled, thinking of the story my dad told me of the time when he was a child up here hunting with his dad, and a couple guys from Stanton came back to camp with three hookers from over in Westwood and half the camp stayed up all night drinking and screwing. And how when they came back from hunting the next morning the women were sunning themselves naked on a big boulder in the meadow and the partying started all over again.

"You think I'm kidding, don't you?" the bartender said. "I shit you not, some guys would come here straight from hunting and drink and play pool for twelve hours. Then be back here the next day hitting it again. Or some guys would come in after dinner and drink five hours worth of beer in an hour." He poured two beers, took a big swallow of one and set the other in front of me.

"And the women would come out of the woodwork. Frustrated housewives whose husbands were off hunting in another zone, groups of gals staying over at Lake Almanor, the whores from Westwood. Sometimes we'd even get hookers from Reno coming over on their days off. They knew a good thing when they saw it."

"Hell," the man continued, pointing to the corner of the bar, "there used to be a slot machine there and one night two guys ripped it right off the wall and ran off with it. They brought it back the next night, apologized, and drank in here for the rest of the season."

"Sounds like I missed out," I said.

"You and me both," he said. "The real wild ones were a big group from some small town down around Sacramento. Shit, what's the name of that town? I can't remember. Anyway."

"Stanton?"

"That's it. Yeah, Stanton. Anyway, by the time I got around to buying this place they all had grown a little long in the tooth. Now I'm lucky if I get five guys in here a night during hunting season."

"Well, I tell you what, if I end up hunting this year, I'll be sure to bring my dad in. I think he'd like this place."

I tried to pay for the second beer but the bartender waved me off. I finished the beer and went to the bathroom. Coming out, I noticed there was a patio out back. The sun was shining high in the sky straight down through the trellis onto clay-fired floor tile. I knelt down and ran my fingers over the Franklin-Martin logo stamped in the corner of a tile, not even having to read it, knowing it purely by its shape.

"I'll be goddamned," I said softly.

I went back into the bar to find the bartender.

"If you're not going to have another one," he said, "I'm going to get back to the snowmobile."

"I'm fine," I said. "That's a nice patio you've got out there."

"Thanks. It doesn't really go with this place much, but a guy from that town I was talking about earlier—Stanton—gave it to the previous owner."

"That was awful nice of him," I said.

The man shrugged. "Guess he wanted to thank the place where he got so many pieces of ass."

"Sounds like a fair trade," I said.

Out on the highway, heading back down to the Sacramento Valley, I turned the radio up high, then turned it off, rolled the windows down then sealed them up tight to block out any noise. The thing was, I didn't really hold it against him. I understood the pull of new pussy, the thought that life was passing you by if you didn't do something bold and adventurous every once in a while. Hell, I wandered occasionally when Melissa and I'd first started dating. And I was past the age where I needed my parents to be my heroes. But still, it's a helluva thing to find out.

I stopped in Gridley and grabbed two Coors Light talls. I was forty-five minutes from home and figured they would ease the ride. Sure enough, I wasn't half way through the first beer when I felt my blood slow down and my skin loosen. What the hell, I thought. If the old man fucked around on my mom, that was between them. Besides, my mom passed four years ago. It's history. Their history, not mine and Melissa's and our child's.

I started work on my house at first light the next weekend. I had the next two weeks off to put in the subfloor, frame the exterior and interior walls, and hang the windows. After that, I was releasing the house to the roofers, plumbers, sheetrockers, and electricians before coming back to take care of the finish carpentry myself.

I was having a work party tomorrow to raise the walls so I had to get the subfloor in place by the end of the day. As I bent down to set the first I-beam in the joist hanger, I heard the intermittent squealing of the brakes on my dad's truck. He believed if you rode the brakes to a stop they'd never last, so he continually pumped them as he came to intersections. And once his brakes went, as they had now, he refused to get new ones for months, and after he did, he'd brag about how long a set of brakes lasted him because he pumped instead of rode.

He walked up the dirt path that would soon be the brick walkway, hunching over and listing forward a bit as he walked. He had on a yellow shirt the color of the polyurethane sealant used on sewer pipe. The front of it read "Sewer Pipe Division: 1875-2002." The back said, "We've been taking shit for over a hundred years."

"My phone must not be working," he said, lightly punching my shoulder.

"I didn't know if you'd be up for it," I said.

"What the hell else would I be doing?"

We started on the north side of the house and proceeded clockwise. The work was simple yet hard. I had set the joist hangers during the week and all that was left was to drop the I-beams in place and nail them to the hangers. But the I-beams were heavy and unwieldy, and after we set a few of them I realized I wouldn't have been able to get them in place without my dad's help. Though he was seventy-six, his arms and shoulders were still strong from a lifetime of work. He had been a foreman his last twenty-five years at the plant, but a foreman at the Pottery was hardly a desk job.

We worked in silence, and I quickly found a rhythm: drive in one nail while reaching for another, then grab a beam and move on. Over and over it went till my vertebrae strained against my skin like fisted knuckles as I bent over and hammered. Sweat slid into my eyes and pulp from the soft Douglas fir settled into the hairs of my forearms, but I didn't stop. I glanced up to see how my dad was keeping up.

"Jesus Christ, you trying to finish the whole house in one day?" he said.

"You're not doing too bad for a senior citizen," I said.

"Like I've always told you, son, the older the buck the harder the horn."

The subfloor was next. We laid down the plywood over the I-beams, and continued to work in silence, save the rhythmic pounding of our hammers. I appreciated the symmetry of construction—the sheetrock on top of the frame, the frame on top of the foundation. You had to build everything plumb from the start and never waver, even though you knew it was impossible. If the cement workers weren't hung-over when they poured the foundation, then the sun warped the wood, or you simply couldn't hold everything square.

My dad went to his truck and came back with a plastic milk jug full of water. He took a big drink, spilling the water on his shirt, then handed it to me, dirty sweat running down its handle. "This is going to be a nice house," he said.

"I meant to thank you for getting me the brick for the walkway."

"No problem. You know how I like to throw my weight around."

I nodded.

"You should've let me get some roof tile, too," he said. "I still have some pull over at the plant, you know."

"It wouldn't go with the design of the house," I said. "Besides, you've done enough already."

"They're practically giving the brick and tile away now," he said. "Every high-rise nowadays is glass and steel. No one wants terra cotta anymore. And all those subdivisions going up in Sacramento, you'd think that'd be great for us, but PVC pipe is so cheap we can't compete, and everyone wants to build cabin-style homes with shake instead of tile roofs, cedar siding instead of brick. If they want a cabin, why don't they move out of the damn city into the mountains?"

"I'm glad you don't work there," he said.

"Hell, Dad, you haven't worked there for ten years, why do you care so much?"

"I just do, I guess."

I handed the jug back to him. "You got one more big push left in you?"

"I taught you everything you know about carpentry, remember?" he said. "But don't forget, son, I didn't teach you everything I know."

I filled my bags with nails. "Need some?" I asked.

He reached into the pouch on his carpenter's belt, jiggled the remaining nails and shook his head. "Heard Robbie and Jack took a ride to Chester the other day. Said they saw three bucks over by Slate Creek. You ever going to go back up hunting?" he asked.

Shit. I had managed to keep the Bambi Inn out of my mind during the entire week, thinking of everything but his affairs. My dad always gave me first shot when we hunted, even after I became an adult, even when he had more hunting days behind him than ahead of him. I never thought about saying no. I wondered if I'd be able to teach my kid about the world even though I've never lived outside of Stanton. And I thought about

134

how being a father probably meant the days of turning away from uncomfortable things were over.

"I'd like to go up again," I said. "What do you say we go up opening weekend?"

"To hunt or just hang out?"

"What the hell's the use of going up there unless you're going to do something?" I said.

"When's the last time you've even shot your rifle?" he asked.

"Doesn't matter," I said. "Hey, maybe we can hit that bar you and all your buddies used to go to all the time when I was little."

"The Bambi Inn? Sure, it beats the hell out of sitting all alone by a campfire."

I looked for signs of hesitation as I threw out the words Bambi Inn, but there were none. All that probably seemed like another lifetime to him. It probably couldn't be explained or regretted over at this point. And I wasn't about to ask for a confession. Besides, this wasn't about the past I kept telling myself, but about the future.

"If you want to go, we'll go," my dad said.

"Who all goes from Stanton anymore?" I asked.

"Robby, Jack, Shorty Stevens. I think sometimes that asshole Mick still goes up."

"Things sure have changed up there, haven't they?" I said.

"Shit, I guess. When I was young there would be twenty families up there. We called Round Valley 'Little Stanton.'"

"Hunt all day, then tear it up all night at the bar," I said. "Doesn't get any better than that."

"You know who were the real wild ones? The Mexicans from the plant. There were almost as many Mexican families up there as us honkys."

"Probably needed to hunt just to feed their families," I said. "Probably wanted something besides tortillas and beans to eat."

My dad snorted. "You think we were any better off than them? Half of our family didn't work during the Depression, and the ones that did had to help support everyone. The years after the Depression were no picnic either. Everything got rationed during the war. The plant didn't pay shit. We needed that meat just as much as anyone. Your Uncle Pete hated to hunt. He'd puke every time he had to gut a deer. It got so bad I finally started gutting his deer for him. But what was he gonna do, let his kids starve?"

"I didn't know any of that," I said, embarrassed of my arrogance, yet grateful to have heard something about my family's history.

My dad shrugged. "It's not something you dwell on while it's happening, and if you're lucky enough to get through it, who the hell wants to relive it."

"If we go up, do you plan on hunting your old stand?" I asked.

"Of course."

I slid my hammer into its loop, letting it dangle against my thigh. "I've got a better idea."

"Such as?"

"Well, those last few years we hunted I scouted that area of Round Valley over by the game refuge."

"I killed a big four-pointer over there road hunting one day with Shorty," my dad said. "Years ago."

"I think the deer have changed their migration pattern because of all the hunting pressure over at Slate Creek. Instead of coming straight down the mountain to where we hunt, they're moving across it towards Round Valley."

"Eric, I can't buck the brush over there. It's too rough. Let's just stay where we've been."

"I'm telling you, Dad, this is a good spot. You can hunt at the bottom of the hill so you won't have to climb."

"And what happens when you shoot one?" he replied quickly, spittle filling the corners of his chapped mouth. "I won't be able to help track it, much less pack it out."

"I can pack it out alone."

"Then what fun is that for me, sitting on a stump like some goddamn statue, hoping a deer comes by and runs into my bullet."

"I was just thinking that this could be our new place."

He waved me off. "I'm too old for new places."

"All the more reason to try. You can get one more big buck."

"Well," I continued when he didn't respond, "if I go, I'm hunting over at Round Valley. And you should too."

"I can't, goddamn it," he shouted.

"That's not my fault," I yelled back. "I want to hunt where the deer are."

"Then let's go out of state, take a guided hunt. I'll pay," he said.

"I can pay my own way."

My dad wiped his mouth, slowly withdrawing his hand as he spoke. "Fine. Fine, fine, fine. You win. We'll hunt wherever you want." He turned away and picked up a piece of plywood.

I watched him nail the plywood to the floor joists, the flesh on the back of his arm loose and shaking as he swung his hammer. I started to tell him about Melissa being pregnant, and how I was sure it was a boy and how I planned to take him hunting. But until he got old enough I would be hunting alone. I grabbed a piece of plywood and decided to hold onto my secret a bit longer, to hold onto the pleasure of its mystery for another day. I bent down and we continued working.

THE BIG EASY

For three songs now this woman who is not his girlfriend has been grinding on Roger. He's in the House of Blues in New Orleans on the final night of a ten-day road trip that began twenty-three hundred miles ago in California. His girlfriend has taken a lectureship position at LSU, and tomorrow Roger will fly back to Stanton and his job with the county.

Bo Diddley is on stage with his box guitar, singing about himself in the third person. "*Bo Diddley, Bo Diddley, do you like my stuff?*" He throws his arms and legs out in time to the beat, movements that would look foolish on a younger man but are decidedly cool when accomplished by a seventy year old. Roger can't deny the press of the woman's breasts against his back or the presence of Linda next to him. But the thing he can't deny the most, the feeling he wishes he was free from, is how goddamn good it feels to have a complete stranger come on to him.

Four songs ago he had felt breath in his ear, a long powerful gust that gave him chills. He'd leaned over to Linda to ask if she was enjoying the show and snuck a look behind him. The woman was smiling at him. She was much older than him, over fifty. Even in the darkness of the club he could see a lifetime of coffee drinking in the stains that framed her teeth. The man next to her was even older and shorter than she was, a bald spot on the crown of his head and thick glasses resting halfway down the bridge of his nose. Roger smiled at the woman. What the hell, he thought.

Then the grinding started. The woman knew every word of every song, and that impressed him because if it wasn't "I'm a Man," or "Who Do You Love," Roger was lost. He pretended to dance to the music, moving against the woman's movements—slightly, gently, undeniably.

The song ended and the grinding stopped. Roger looked back and saw only the man, giving him a friendly nod, then sliding Linda's empty cup inside his and squeezing his way to the bar. The woman was already there. He leaned into her, over her, as if he had every right to, and ordered.

"How are you?" he asked, trying to sound casual.

"You dance good," she said. She had on rings and bracelets and necklaces that jangled as she spoke.

"Speaking of that, where is a good place to go dancing?" he asked, putting his mouth almost on her ear.

She bent him down to her level with a firm hand on his neck. He liked the feel of her fingertips on his skin. "Tipitina's. The original one. But if you want to people watch, you can't beat the balcony at The Cat's Meow," she said.

"Where's that?" he asked.

"On Bourbon Street."

"What isn't?" he said and laughed.

"You'll find it," she said.

The show was over soon after he got back to Linda with their drinks, and the crowd immediately began filing out.

"Haven't these people ever heard of an encore?" Linda said.

"Rookies!" Roger shouted.

But there was no encore. After ten minutes of waiting, when they turned to leave, Roger was not surprised to find that the woman was gone. Just as well, he thought, what the hell could I have done? But still….

He and Linda had been dating only three months when she got the job offer from LSU at the beginning of the summer, and when she told him about it she said that she'd always wanted to drive across the country and how much fun they would have on the trip. That's the way she was, to the point but always leaving something out, something implied that Roger had to fill in to understand her. Their few disagreements had stemmed from the times he couldn't make the connections between what she had said and what she had meant. She had been teaching at the junior college in the next town over and had moved to Stanton because rents were cheaper. They'd met when Roger did a flood survey on her house for insurance purposes. The next week they ran into each other at the Stanton Inn and after a night of darts and house whiskey, they woke up naked on her living room floor and had been together ever since.

On the drive out to Louisiana he learned that he couldn't speak against her sister, that she spoke freely about her long-term ex-boyfriend and demanded that he do the same about his ex-girlfriend. Our present is a conglomeration of our past, she said somewhere in Oklahoma, and our future grows out of decisions we make in the present.

Remarks like that reinforced his initial impression that she was different from most Stanton women. It wasn't just the education, but what she had gone through to get the education: growing up in Arizona, going to college in Los Angeles, then grad school in Oregon. He knew plenty of smart people in town and a diploma had nothing to do with it, but it was the going away, the mindset to want to leave and then actually doing it, that set her apart.

Most of the land surveying Roger did was either in Stanton or in the nearby towns of Wheatland, Sheridan, or Nicolaus that were even smaller than Stanton, and he had steadfastly refused to believe that life was that much different outside the borders of his hometown. That way he was neither awed by Sacramento, which lay just thirty miles southwest of Stanton, nor bitter about still being in Stanton. But Linda was putting cracks in those beliefs.

After the concert, they went to Pat O'Brien's for Hurricanes and so Roger could buy a souvenir glass. Linda held onto his arm with both hands as they walked to the patio, pulling him into her.

"Babe, you're knocking me over," he said.

"You've already bowled me over," she said.

He laughed. "Very smooth. Don't worry, you'll get one last throw for the road before I leave."

Linda ordered a second Hurricane as Roger paid for his glass and some packaged Hurricane mix. She had already sucked half of it down by the time they got to their hotel on Chartres and Dumaine. She stood against the wall as Roger opened the door, her lipstick shiny from the light of the streetlamp above them, her eyes wet and warm. He kissed her hard, and they fell against the wall. He was a few inches taller and at least fifty pounds heavier than she was, but when she held him tight he was powerless.

Inside, she finished off her drink before he had undressed.

"You're going big fly tonight," Roger said.

"If not tonight, when?" she said.

He shrugged, unsure of what she meant.

"I'm sad," she said.

He was too, but she had deemed this trip to be the end of them without asking his opinion, so he felt that she didn't have the right to be sad.

"Come lay with me," she said.

He swallowed his objection and went to her. She was warm and relaxed like she'd just woken from an afternoon nap. They wrapped around each other and wordlessly stroked each other's arms, back, and neck. She was asleep in minutes. He slid from her grasp and went to the bathroom. The trip had been everything he'd expected: road head on I-5 a half hour into the drive, hiking the Grand Canyon, the Cadillac Ranch in Amarillo, Beale Street and Graceland in Memphis, and now the French Quarter. The only thing left was for him to leave.

Somewhere around Fort Smith, Arkansas, Roger realized that part of Linda's willingness to talk about her past and to hear about his was because she had no fear of what it might do them in the future. New Orleans would be as far as they would go together. There was still too much that was unknown between them, too much to straddle the distance that would soon separate them.

He dug a condom out of his bag, splashed water on his face and looked at his reflection in the mirror. "You're a bastard," he said. He quickly slipped out of the room and was back into the madness that is the French Quarter on a Friday night: flashers, freaks, drunks, gawkers. People without a care in the world, and people with too many. He was unable to get out of the way of a very large, very drunk woman wearing a tie-dyed tank top with no bra, black spandex pants, and silver glitter in her hair. He asked her about The Cat's Meow and she thrust her arm out proudly like a palace guard and directed him to it.

The woman was at the back corner of the bar; he saw her illuminated perfectly by the outside streetlights as he entered the club. Roger was both fearful and excited that she must somehow know his every weakness, that she had appeared tonight not to test him, but to expose him.

"Buy an out-of-towner a drink?" Roger said as he approached her.

She signaled for the bartender and looked at Roger as if deciding if she still wanted him now that he was here in the flesh.

"Enjoy the concert?" Roger asked.

"Couldn't you tell?" she said, sliding a fresh whiskey sour over to him. Her rings and bracelets were gone.

He touched his glass to hers and leaned against the bar, the crowd in front of him, the woman in the corner of his eye. He hated these situations. He'd slept with a handful of older women, some who by now must be older than the one next to him. He was no pretty boy, but he had a fairly flat belly, all his hair, and no crow's feet around the eyes, making him look younger than his thirty-two years.

He never knew how the women wanted him to act. Did they want a young, carefree, joke-telling, shot-pounding, baby-why-don't-you-come-along-for-the-ride kind of guy who'd help them forget how old they were, or did they not want to be reminded of the difference in their ages, wanted someone to be like their husband, just not *be* their husband? Not knowing which play to make made him nervous because there were no second chances on nights like this. He at least knew that much.

He pounded his drink. "Do you have a room here in the French Quarter?" he asked the woman, looking her directly in the eye. This was the second and final thing he knew: You had to look them in the eye when you asked such a question. She was smiling but her eyes were motionless. Not dull, but they seemed to be taking Roger in rather than projecting herself out to him.

"What state are you from?" she asked.

"California," he said.

"Figures. It's called the Quarter, not the French Quarter. And it's N'Awlins, not New Or-leans."

"Not everyone surfs in California, you know," he said.

The woman grabbed his hand with such a light touch he wasn't sure she had grabbed him until they were moving through the bar. They stopped a block later and kissed right in the middle of Bourbon Street, supreme privacy among hundreds of strangers floating by.

"My name's Roger," he said when they resumed walking.

"Good for you," she said.

Inside her hotel room, he reached for her as soon as she closed the door, before she had a chance to hit the lights. He was fully aware of what he was doing; he didn't need anything illuminated further. They kissed, he kissing harder than her, and she went for his pants. They stumbled onto the bed and Roger reached for his condom while undressing with his free hand. This had to be done quickly or not at all.

The woman braced her palms against his chest. "Tell me something about yourself," she said.

Give me a break, he thought. "Okay," he nodded. "My name's Roger. I live in California. I'm a land surveyor for the county."

"Tell me about you," she said, holding her hands firm against him.

He took a deep breath. "I think free enterprise is anything but free for most of the workers of this country. I think being able to keep a secret is the best trait a friend can have. And I really don't get the popularity of NASCAR."

"And?" she said.

"And what?" he said.

"You tell me," she said.

"I volunteer for Habitat for Humanity, help build houses for poor people," he said.

"Tell me something bad you've done, something you're ashamed of."

"Why?"

146

"It's what we do wrong that tells us who we are. How much you will betray yourself, and how you live with whatever you've done, that's the true measure of who you are."

"Is that some Cajun/voodoo philosophy?" he said, laughing.

"Tell me," she said and he quit laughing. She didn't seem the least bit drunk anymore.

"Okay," he said, and she slid her hands from his chest to his back and he fell softly into her.

But she spoke before he had a chance. "Once, probably twenty-five years ago, I was flat broke. My two best friends, Jackie and Dana, were the only things that kept me sane. They helped me look for a job, wouldn't let me get depressed. One Sunday we went out to brunch. They paid my way, of course. After all the champagne at brunch we ended up at Dana's place where we ordered a pizza and bought some wine. It was one of the best days of my life, sitting around talking and drinking with my two best friends. I can't remember how many times I cried from laughing that day."

Her eyelashes brushed against Roger's, his lips so close to hers that he was sucking in the carbon dioxide coming out with her words. He squirmed to signal his discomfort but she held him tight.

"They both passed out by the eleven o'clock news," she continued, "and I gathered my purse and keys to go, wondering if I had enough gas to get home, wondering if I had enough money to buy gas. The kitchen table had three empty bottles of wine and two pizza boxes on it. I can still see all the uneaten crust in the boxes because none of us liked it. In the middle of all that mess was Dana and Jackie's change from the day. There were six ones, four fives, a ten, and forty-eight cents of change. I took a five and the ten."

"Did you ever tell them?" Roger asked.

"That's not a story you tell loved ones," she said. He rolled onto his side facing her but when he began speaking he turned from her gaze, looking into the darkness of the room, looking at nothing.

147

"Six, seven years ago, my Godfather was seriously ill. My mom would tell me I should go and see him but I never did, even though he lived just across town. He was a very cool guy, gave me my first St. Christopher, my first baseball glove. He always bought me Christmas and birthday presents, even though I never did for him. He had this way about him that put you at ease. I got grounded once in high school for drinking and complained to him about how unfair my parents were being. 'I didn't do anything my dad didn't do when he was my age,' I said. 'And he didn't do anything to you that his dad didn't do to him,' he said. Just like that he made me see where my parents were coming from without making me feel like an asshole. Anyway, I never went to see him. And then he died. I was a pallbearer at the funeral but it all felt too little too late."

Roger climbed on top of the woman. "He was so cool. I wish I'd told him that. I wish I'd told someone that."

They kissed and he slipped the condom on. "Don't worry," he said, "I'm using protection."

She smiled and ran her hand over his hair. "Oh, honey, getting pregnant is the last thing I'm worried about."

Me, too, he wanted to say, but figured now was not the time for insults.

He finished quickly. He knew when he thought about this later, he wouldn't remember anything about what the woman looked like, the color of her skin, the texture of her lips. He rolled off her and went to the bathroom to dispose of the condom.

"Can I get you anything?" he said. "Tissue, a glass of water?"

"I'm fine," she said.

He came back and sat on the edge of the bed, a hand on her thigh, hoping she didn't want him under the covers. "You can go," she said.

"That's okay, I got some time," he said.

"I think we've done all we set out to do," she said.

"I guess."

"Thank you," she said, touching the small of his back.

"Anytime," he said.

148

The next day, as Roger and Linda went from booth to booth in the French Market after beignets at Café Du Monde, Linda wondered aloud if he was okay. "It's not like you to be this quiet," she said, holding up a baby alligator skull for his inspection.

He had never been around so many people for so long a time. The trips down to the Bay Area to watch a Raider or A's game were hectic, but at least the car ride there and back provided a few hours of solitude between the constant noise and jostling of the crowd. Strangely, he felt a sense of intimacy with Linda within the chaos of New Orleans, like they were traveling out of the country and he could say anything because no one around them could speak their language.

He kissed her. "Maybe I'm sad, too," he said.

She pressed against him and leaned her head back for a kiss, a movement of such sincere wanting and vulnerability he wondered why he was getting on a plane and leaving in four hours. He thought of how the most thrilling part of being with that woman last night had been the time before he was actually with her, and how she wasn't nearly thrilling enough to override the disgust he felt with himself. Linda would never know, but every time he thought back on their trip he'd have to include last night, and he'd be reminded of how easy he was in all the wrong ways, how quick he was to give way.

After he bought a T-shirt that said *Louisiana: It's not the Heat, it's the Stupidity,* they ate muffulettas at Napoleon House and got a Jell-O shot of Everclear.

"This city is unreal. It's like Club Med for hedonists," he said.

Back at their hotel she undressed him, then herself, and gave him a full body massage with her own body, rubbing over him like a snake. He lay on his stomach, eyes shut tight, trying to feel and not think, trying to remember her smell, her contours.

"Make love to me," she whispered in his ear.

He rolled over and they kissed for a long time. He finally pulled away and said, "Tell me something about you that I don't know. Something you did and wouldn't want to do again, but still might."

"Something to remember me by, huh?" she said. She was lying completely on top of him, her hair in his eyes. She grabbed her hair and held it in a bun behind her head.

"You first. You must have a story you want to tell," she said.

"Not really," he said, but one came to him instantly. "Once I fooled around with a friend's girlfriend. It went on for about seven months. He never found out. She wanted to tell him, get everything out in the open. I said no way. I was content to keep sneaking over to her house once a week."

"Is he still your friend?"

"He moved to Nevada three years ago with a woman he met in traffic school. But I still consider him a friend."

"And you never told him, even after all this time?" she asked.

He shut his eyes to her. "I didn't see how that would help anyone. That girl was out of the picture for both of us, and he married another woman. Besides, that's not the point at all."

"When I was in college I fooled around on my ex and caught crabs," Linda said. "As I was about to tell him about the affair, he confesses that he's been screwing around on me, and he's sorry he gave me crabs."

"Get out," Roger said.

"I hung it over his head until he was so ashamed he asked me to marry him."

"I knew this woman who was so broke she stole money from her best friends," Roger said.

"My cousin paid someone to take the SAT for him," Linda said. "He had a scholarship to play baseball and needed an 800 to qualify. He got an 850 on the pre-test but was afraid the stress of the real test might make him give up the fifty points."

They began laughing, louder and longer until they were crying. They gradually stopped, dabbing their eyes with tissues, then started up all over again before stopping for good. Then they made love.

After, Linda closed her eyes and put her head on Roger's chest. He caressed her hair. They would have to get ready to leave soon. The room was closed tight, dark and quiet, and he wanted nothing more than to stay tucked away with her.

Linda's breath took on the rhythm of sleep. One of her shoulders had a small bone sticking up in the middle of it that dug into Roger's ribs. He ran his hand along the other shoulder but it was smooth. He held her, humbled by all the things he was capable of doing, wondering if he would eventually become those things.

Outside, the Quarter was starting up again, rumbling like a powerful engine turning over, a joyous celebration about to explode. He went to the window and pulled back the curtain. A shaft of light split the room. He wondered how long it would take before he felt joyous again.

EMPLOYEE OF THE YEAR

Richard decided to put his brother on a forklift shuttling terra cotta from the fitting shed to the shipping yard. He thought it would suit Tommy because he would never be in one place long enough to be supervised closely, yet there would always be time at each pick up and drop off to bullshit with the other workers. The Pottery was thirty acres of kilns, sheds, and open space. The main factory—where the clay was molded by machines that didn't stop moving from six in the morning until two-thirty in the afternoon—was connected to the Lincoln and Cordova kilns, where the products were fired, and speed seal, where the pipe was given its polyurethane sealant. In all, the three departments were under a building almost two football fields long. The maintenance department, personnel, fitting shed, clay prep, and shipping and receiving had their own buildings throughout the plant. As foreman of the shipping and receiving department, Richard would see Tommy periodically and hoped if any screw-ups occurred they would be out of his sight.

Richard had run through all the scenarios that could turn the idea of his brother working at the Pottery to shit. One, there was the plant manager, Frank Hollins, whose management style consisted of yelling or really yelling. Then there was Tommy himself. No telling how he'd respond to having to show up on time to the same place five days a week, especially if that place was the Pottery. But a condition of his probation was gainful employment, and the Pottery was the biggest company in a small town.

Richard had gone to work at the Pottery the Monday after graduating from high school sixteen years ago. He showed up at six in the morning and by six-thirty was stacking brick onto a pallet. The plant had fed and clothed three generations of families in Stanton by firing clay into brick and tile and pipe, and stepping outside of that reality had never seriously occurred to Richard.

But it had occurred to Tommy from the moment he could speak. He'd tell anyone who would listen that he wouldn't be another wetback working at the Pottery. He worked construction after high school and when he'd start in on what a shitty place the Pottery was, Richard would shoot back that construction wasn't any better and he should be a little more grateful because it was the Pottery that had put a roof over their heads and food on their table when they were kids. Richard would hear himself say those things and think, my god, I sound like an old man. But then, Tommy had a way of making everyone around him seem more conservative than they really were. He lived a life with seemingly so few consequences that it was hard not to sit in judgment. And even when things did go south on him, like when he was put away for a year, he never pissed and moaned about it.

Richard wasn't foolish enough to believe that injecting structure into his brother's life would suddenly make the drug dealing, bookmaking, and lord-knows-what-else go away. He was simply playing the odds. Left to his own devices, Tommy had too much energy, too sharp of a tongue, too strong of a belief in his own desires not to find trouble. But, Richard reasoned, if he could keep him busy five out of seven days, well, he'd take those odds. And since it was his little brother, it was a bet he'd lay down every day of the week.

Richard drove into the plant at ten till six, passing workers leaning against the brick walls of the kilns, warming themselves in the cool spring morning. He almost didn't recognize Tommy when he saw him at the time clock outside the fitting shed, the blaze in his eyes dull behind safety glasses, his ponytail hidden away under a yellow hardhat.

The whistle blew at five till the hour, and the workers hurried to their posts, flinging coffee onto the hardpan dirt that served as the floor of the plant and grinding out cigarettes with steel toe boots. The air crackled with the sound of forklift engines being turned over and the whirring of wet saws in the fitting shed. In the main factory, machines that squeezed out molds of brick and tile were turned on, awaiting a simple mixture of clay and water. The heavy clang of the Lincoln kiln's

156

steel doors opening in anticipation of a car of pipe echoed in the yard.

Richard went into the personnel office for a cup of coffee and ran into Frank Hollins. They nodded hello and walked outside. Hollins lit a cigar, his last one of the workday, after which he'd smoke until he went to bed. He resented having to go without a cigar for those eight hours and seemed to blame the workers for his need.

"Tommy Sanchez," he said. "I hope you know what you're doing, *Ricardo*. Your brother's one *loco hombre*."

"Hell, he ain't even the wildest one here at the plant," Richard said. He was always a little insulted whenever he heard Hollins' butchered accent. Most of the plant's workers were Mexican, and Hollins was just trying to get along, but still, Richard thought, if you're going to speak another person's language, you ought to respect it enough to do it well.

Hollins spit out bits of cigar leaf with two flicks of his tongue and licked his lips. "You're probably right. Ain't that a sad fucking commentary on this place?"

He pointed his cigar at Richard. "Here's the difference, though. A lot of these guys are wild because they're stupid, but your brother's uncontrollable. No fear and just a shred too much pride."

"Family and business," he said when Richard didn't reply.

"Are you kidding me, Frank? That's all that's in this place. Without nepotism we couldn't fill out a crew."

"And look where it's gotten us. Having to carry a bunch of sorry asses because if we fired them their cousin or uncle or dad would pout like a baby without their tit."

"Or cigar."

Hollins licked his lips again, then smiled with a quick upturn of his mouth. "You're a white hat now, Richard. No matter which way you turn there's always someone looking right at you."

"Oh, Christ, Frank. Don't you think I know that? Don't you think I'm better than that?"

"Family changes everything."

"Yeah, well, sometimes you got no choice."

Hollins laughed. "This is Stanton, *Ricardo*. Look around. No one's here because they want to be."

"You sound like an expert."

Hollins walked a few steps toward his office then stopped. "Rumor is he knocked up my niece a few years back. No one knows for sure and she ain't saying. She lives over in Jackson now, has a good job, got her life together. I don't hold grudges, Richard, but watch yourself. Remember what's important."

Richard saw Jerry Boyle coming towards them. He had recently been promoted out of the personnel office to head of the clay prep division. Usually working in personnel is where the Pottery put white hats at the end of their time, or where a white hat with no ambition other than to keep his hat clean requested to go. The personnel office was next to Hollins' office, meaning Boyle had had Hollins' ear most of the day for the past year and had managed to leap from a yellow hat in personnel to a white hat for one of the six main divisions of the plant.

"I need to go check on yesterday's shipment," Richard said and walked away.

Tommy ate lunch with the other forklift drivers that first day. He had just picked up a pallet of terra cotta when the whistle blew at five till eleven. Hector Banuelos motioned for him to leave it.

"*Comer*," he said, putting his hand to his mouth.

"Hey, I may be a *pocho* but I ain't no fucking *gavacho*," Tommy said, hopping off his forklift. "*Entiendes*?" He had a rat-a-tat way of speaking, an urgent rhythm that made everything he said sound as if he were both bullshitting and relaying rare insights all at once.

The first thing Tommy did as he stood in line to punch out for lunch was to take off his hat, undo his ponytail and shake out his hair. All the buildings had large open bays so product could be moved easily from one place to the next. Because of the kilns, the inside of the Pottery was ten degrees hotter than the rest of town so at lunch workers either fled to the convenience store across the street or found shelter in the shade of a bay.

Highway 65 and downtown Stanton were visible from the fitting shed; the Pottery was visible from most any part of town, so it seemed the town and the plant were in a perpetual staring contest. Banuelos sat next to Tommy as they ate in the bay of the fitting shed. His face was dark and creased under the eyes, around the mouth, even the cheeks, and his gray stubble looked as if it could cut glass. Tommy and Richard's father had told them stories about Banuelos, how he came over from Michoacán at sixteen—a half-Indian from the mountains of Mexico—and when he started at the plant no one could keep up with him setting pipe on the Lincoln kiln. Now, he sat on a forklift all day and drank for hours after work in the parking lot of the 7-Eleven. His wife didn't mind, their father had told them, because they had six children and Banuelos had a pecker the size of a loaf of bread, so anything that kept him out of the house was fine with her.

"*Cómo esta tu madre?*" he asked Tommy.

"*Duro.*"

Banuelos laughed and held out a taco for Tommy. Tommy held up his own taco.

"Watch out for Blow Up," one of the men said. "He's a screamer."

"Hollins," another man said when Tommy didn't register the nickname.

Banuelos looked around and leaned close to Tommy. "*No le gusta.* Thinks we're all his *mayates*," he said and pinched Tommy's skin until it turned from brown to red.

"Don't forget about Boyle," another man said. "He is Hollins' *mayate.*"

"You'll do okay," Banuelos said to Tommy. "You're a good boy. You don't remember me, huh?"

"A little bit."

"I used to work on your dad's car. Remember that old Chevy?"

"I hear you have a pecker as big as a loaf of bread," Tommy said.

The other men stopped eating. "*Qué?*" said Banuelos.

"*Cojones grande,*" Tommy said, holding his hands a foot apart.

The men laughed. One of them slapped Tommy on the back.

"*Sí, carnal,*" Banuelos said. "*Mucho grande.*"

"Let's see it, then," Tommy said.

Banuelos waggled his finger at him. "*Solamente para las mujeres, mijo.*"

"Whip that hog out," Tommy said. "If it's as big as everyone says, you ought to be proud of it."

"Yeah."

"Come on, I've heard about it for twenty years. I want to see it."

Someone knocked Banuelos on the shoulder and he leaped up like he'd touched a piece of brick just pulled from the kiln.

"*Listo?*" he asked.

"*Orale!*" the men roared.

He smiled and reached deep into his pants and pulled out the longest, skinniest loaf of bread any of them had ever seen.

"*Chinga me.*"

"*Dios mio.*"

Tommy laughed until tears blurred his vision as Banuelos grinned and pivoted so every man could see it.

"Okay, okay" Tommy said. "Put that thing away, *maricón.*"

Banuelos' face turned soft. "You're the one who wanted to see it."

Richard found Tommy at the end of the day and saw, as the time clock snapped down on his time card, a look of astonishment on his brother's face that anyone would take a job where they had to keep track of their time. But it was this or back to

County, and Richard knew Tommy would do anything to keep his freedom, no matter how neutered it was.

He idled his truck next to Tommy and their cousin Road Runner. "Hop in *pendejos*. I'm buying."

"Don't worry about us, white hat," Tommy said. "We're going to walk out with the real workers."

"But we will let you buy the first round," Road Runner said.

There were a dozen workers who drank every day at the 7-Eleven, and on Fridays that number swelled to almost fifty. The once-a-week drinkers would pull their trucks close to the side of the store and sit on their tailgates, letting the regulars have their reserved spots against the side of the building. Richard and Tommy's father was a Friday drinker, staying later and later as the years passed. Most of the workers at the Pottery were straight from Mexico or *pochos* with the sweat of the fields still on them. They thought it was a natural transition, from picking what came out of the ground to creating something with that same ground, and most believed they had moved up a notch on the scale of things.

Richard often thought that his dad and the other men drank at first because they had it so good in America, then later they drank because they realized this would be all they would get. It was a question never asked and an answer never offered, and now it was too late for either.

Their dad worked on the Lincoln kiln for thirty-five years, setting twelve and sixteen-inch sewer pipe. It kept him strong for many of those years then made him old overnight. He started coughing up blood a month before his fifty-seventh birthday and didn't live to see his fifty-eighth. Richard wondered what his dad would think of him becoming a white hat so soon. He'd be happy, sure, but would he be a little resentful or think that it was the natural progression of things, that that was why he had left Juarez for Ysleta, Texas, and, finding it no better just across the border, worked his way to Northern California? Richard had an uncomfortable feeling that he, Richard, would be a little jealous if his son surpassed him so quickly, that success shouldn't be so easy.

Richard had a twelve-pack of beer waiting for Tommy and Road Runner, but Tommy insisted on buying a second one. He came out of the store and handed beers out like presents at Christmastime.

"Here," he said as he gave Banuelos a sixteen-ounce Budweiser. "I got you a tall boy."

"I hear you had him parading around all naked at lunch," Richard said when Tommy rejoined him and Road Runner at the truck. Richard knew Tommy would fit right in at the plant. He was so cocksure of the way he was living he was like a thunderstorm that wipes away the haze of an overcast day. That's why people liked him so much, especially in Stanton, where ambitions were often set by who you were related to or how good of a football player you were in high school.

"If I had a tool like that I'd be in the movies," Tommy said.

"Hasn't that little one of yours gotten you in enough trouble?" Road Runner said.

"Hey, when I knock up a woman it'll be because I want to," Tommy said. "I don't give a shit what Hollins thinks."

"Your reputation precedes you, I guess," Richard said between drinks. "Isn't that what you've always wanted?"

"Believe me, I've got enough going on without getting blamed for shit I don't do."

One of the men gave them some tacos left over from lunch and Richard handed him a beer.

"This is as good as it gets, *carnal*," Road Runner said. "Steady work that don't break your back and cold *cervezas* after work."

"Shit, if I'm still here in twenty years put a fucking bullet in my head," Tommy said.

"Listen to your cousin," Richard said, holding up his beer in a toast. "There are a lot worse ways to make a living."

"Oh, oh," Road Runner said. "*Ricardo* sounds like a lifer."

162

"You think they're going to let you run this place one day, brother?" Tommy asked.

"I don't know," Richard said. "But I'm going to make them say no." Richard hadn't realized he felt that way until he said the words out loud. But there it was, his future for everyone to know.

"This is a way to make money," Tommy said. "It sure ain't no way to live, but you wetbacks don't get the difference."

For all his talk about work being for suckers, Tommy was a good worker. He wasn't fast, or full of manic energy as Richard had expected—but was as steady as the whistles that sounded eight times a day throughout the plant. And he never called in sick, which, in a place where almost twenty percent of the workers called in sick on Mondays or Fridays, put him on the short list for any upcoming promotions after only six months. Tommy's weekends still started on Thursday and didn't end until Sunday night, but he always managed to be in front of the time clock at six a.m. Monday through Friday. Their father had told them when they were young that a man could drink all he wanted but should be prepared to back up anything he said while drunk. If not, then he was just a stupid wetback. And whatever Tommy thought of himself, he definitely didn't think of himself as stupid or a wetback.

Work wasn't without its hiccups. Hollins yelled at everyone for any slip up; it didn't matter if the mistake was big or small, the volume was the same, and eventually he got around to Tommy. Tommy had failed to sound his horn going around a corner and ran into another forklift, ruining a load of terra cotta.

Richard found Hollins afterwards. "I'd appreciate it if you'd let me discipline my workers," he said.

"I ain't got time to run around looking for people when shit needs to be handled," Hollins replied.

"I don't have a problem dealing with my brother as an employee," Richard said.

"That's fine, Richard," Hollins said. "But I'm the plant manager. All these guys are my workers, *comprende?*"

Richard went to Tommy and told him he was sorry for the bitching Hollins had given him.

"Fuck him," Tommy said. "When's the last time he did any work?"

"I know. He always goes overboard," Richard said.

"I honked, by the way."

"I believe you."

"Fuck him," Tommy said again. He had that look in his eyes, as if contemplating what would be the most extreme way to blow up the situation he was in. "When's the last time he did any real work?"

"Exactly," Richard said.

Finally, Tommy shrugged. "I guess that's the job, right? Either take the shit or leave."

"That's about right."

"Not great options, brother."

"But still, options, brother."

At the end of the summer the Pottery was celebrating one hundred years in business with a company-wide party at the Memorial Auditorium in downtown Sacramento. The truss division from Dixon, the brick company in south Sacramento, and the lumber mill from Hayfork were all being bussed in as the plant shut down at noon on a Friday.

Tommy and Road Runner came over to meet up with Richard, pulling up on a brand new Harley.

"Doesn't that thing hurt your ass?" Richard asked.

"What are you talking about?"

"From being so hot."

Road Runner punched Tommy in the shoulder. "He got you on that one."

"Let's just say a guy owed me a favor, and this is how he repaid me," Tommy said. "And that's all you need to know."

"You're a regular pillar of the business community," Richard said.

Road Runner laughed. "Yeah, what's next, joining the chamber of commerce?"

"Keep laughing, *pendejos,*" Tommy said. "The vig on your bets just went up to twenty percent."

When Road Runner went to use the bathroom Tommy turned to Richard. "We need to keep him half-ass sober today. His old lady said if he comes home all messed up again he's out the door. And I don't want his ugly ass sleeping on my couch again."

Richard nodded.

"All right," Tommy said when Road Runner returned. "Let's go show off our Saturday-night personalities."

"How do you think that little squid Boyle will be today?" Road Runner said as they drove to the 7-Eleven to meet the buses.

"Any way Hollins wants him to be," Richard said. "Just like always."

"He gives me a bad feeling," Road Runner said. "He'd sell all three of us out in a minute."

Road Runner and Tommy had been down on Boyle since Road Runner had called in sick one Monday and Boyle told Hollins that he had seen Road Runner's truck up at the Oasis the night before. Hollins ended up docking him a day's pay.

"Come on," Richard said. "We all know he's a candy-ass, but how would you like to be Hollins' boy all day at work then go home to Caroline? Have her constantly sticking a cattle prod up your ass to do more, get promoted faster."

"I don't give a shit," Road Runner said. "That's no reason for him to get in my business."

"Yeah," Tommy said from the back seat. "No one told him to become Hollins' bitch and no one told him to marry that hole."

"Just don't deal with the *maricón,* then," Richard said, knowing a losing argument when he was in one.

"It ain't always that easy," Road Runner said.

"And it's what happens after you deal with him that screws everything up," Tommy said.

They drove through the four-block downtown of Stanton, past banners on every storefront proclaiming the plant's centennial.

"The town sure got excited about this," Richard said, wanting to change the subject.

"Drinking and fucking and gossiping, that's all there's to do in this town," Tommy said. "I do the first two and have the third one done to me."

There were six buses in all—plain white—so when they pulled out of the 7-Eleven they resembled a string of pearls cutting through town.

The Memorial Auditorium was an orgy of food and drink and games. The tables of food were arranged by theme: seafood, Mexican, Italian, Chinese. Tommy, Road Runner, and Richard took over an hour to circle the room, stopping at each keg to top off their cups and tasting from every food station. A quick, informal meeting was held in which Boyle was named Employee of the Year and then it was back to partying.

They hit golf balls into a net, shot baskets, and threw a baseball that registered how hard they threw. Tommy won at seventy-two miles per hour. A Beatles tribute band played in the middle of the room on a revolving stage. After a game of darts they broke for more food and drink.

"Give me one of those," Road Runner said when Tommy came back with beers. Richard had that dangerous buzz where it felt too good to stop but wouldn't take much to spill him over into complete drunkenness. His brother and cousin never seemed to ponder that choice, electing to dive headlong over that cliff. Road Runner went to the bathroom and Richard looked at Tommy.

"He's fine. He ain't a lightweight like you," Tommy said.

"My wife ain't going to kick me out if I come home shitty."

"Denise may not either. Or maybe she will. He knows the score," Tommy said.

"I thought we were supposed to help him?"

"We are, by letting him be a grown-ass man."

166

It was dark when they left, hours lost to drinking and eating and walking the auditorium. Everyone's faces were shiny and their hair matted with sweat. They opened all the windows in the bus and sped back down Highway 80. Richard settled into his seat, drunk and tired and wanting to be home.

Tommy's voice came bursting from the back of the bus. "Richard! Get your ass back here and drink with us."

He and Road Runner had dragged an ice chest into the middle of the aisle in back, blocking the way to the bathroom. Richard pretended not to hear his brother.

"*Ricardo!*" Tommy shouted again. His voice was an intrusion, a challenge.

Hollins and Boyle looked toward the back of the bus. Richard stayed put.

"Fine. Stay up there with all the other white hats, you candy-ass," Tommy said. He opened a beer, drank a third of it at once, wiped his chin and leaned forward, peering toward the front of the bus.

"Hey, Banuelos, who'd you vote for for Employee of the Year?" Tommy asked. The bus went quiet. No air swirled through the open windows; the tires hushed against the freeway.

"Huh?" Banuelos said, half passed out.

"You heard me, *pieto grande*, who'd you vote for?" Tommy was mumbling but everyone understood what he was saying.

"Richard," Banuelos said.

"Ortiz, how 'bout you?"

"None of your business."

"Shut the hell up back there," Hollins yelled.

"Myself, I voted for Road Runner," Tommy said. "I think he would've won if he hadn't got docked that one day's pay."

Hollins stood up. "I said shut the hell up, Sanchez. We're almost home. You can talk all you want then."

"Ortiz," Tommy said calmly. "This ain't no secret fucking ballot. Who'd you vote for?"

"Banuelos," he said softly and the weight of the bus shifted to the back. As the other men offered up Banuelos as their choice for employee of the year, Richard rubbed his face hard, wishing he were sober. Tommy questioned everyone on the bus and Boyle's name wasn't uttered once.

Suddenly, Hollins was in Tommy's face, all puffed up like a banty rooster. "You two are dumber than you look."

"Just taking a poll, *jefe,*" Tommy said.

"Keep talking, Sanchez. You're real fucking funny."

"Just blowing off some steam, boss," Tommy said.

"Well, I don't like it," Hollins said, leaning over Tommy, who was still seated. His face was hard but some of the anger was gone, like he thought he had Tommy down.

"Then go back up front," Tommy said. "What the fuck are you doing back here anyway?"

"Trying to keep you assholes in line." Hollins was all puffed up again. Faces poked out into the aisle, still and quiet like masks with no bodies attached. Boyle was on his knees in his seat up front so he could see over the men. Road Runner stared at Tommy as if waiting for a signal.

"We ain't causing any trouble, Mr. Boss Man," Tommy said.

"If you want to get drunk and stir up shit you know nothing about, go ahead. I just don't want to hear it the rest of the trip."

"Then don't listen." This time it was Road Runner. If Tommy's attitude was one of defiance, Road Runner's was pure anger. He looked ready to spring for Hollins' throat.

Hollins stiffened a bit then puffed back out, though not as far as before, as if he had weighed the challenge in Road Runner's voice.

"Fine. Just keep drinking, boys. Road Runner, maybe when you get home Denise will kick your ass out."

Tommy stood up. He was half a head taller than Hollins. "Why'd you have to ruin it?" he said. "You should've stayed up front with your boy where you belong and just let us blow off some steam."

"We'll take this off the bus if you want when we get back, but until then I want you two quiet," Hollins said.

"All of you," Hollins said, walking back to his seat. "I want everyone to shut the hell up."

They were on the last bus into town. The traffic lights were blinking and the only cars out were those parked at the Oasis. The smokestacks of the Pottery stood silent and rigid in the night, as if on guard. The 7-Eleven was empty, and the bus driver pulled in and stopped sideways, eager to be rid of his passengers.

Richard let Banuelos slide out of the seat past him. "I need to talk to my brother," he said.

"You should talk to Hollins instead," Banuelos said. "He's the only one you can reason with."

"*Estás borracho,*" Richard told him.

"*Sí, sí,*" Banuelos said, staggering down the aisle. "*Siempre, siempre, siempre.*"

Richard walked back to Tommy. "Do you think our old man traveled all that way, and worked all those years to have you go backwards?"

"Do you think he traveled all this way to be somebody's *mayate*?"

"Let this go," Richard said. "I can't back you."

"I never asked you to," Tommy said.

"You'll wind up back in jail."

"He shits on everyone, *Ricardo*. He shit all over Banuelos," Tommy said.

"So let Banuelos deal with it."

"Fuck!" Tommy yelled and moved quickly past Richard.

The men milled around to see what would happen. But Richard knew before it happened. He walked to his car as Tommy, Road Runner, Hollins, and Boyle started jawing about what had transpired on the bus. Their voices grew louder as Richard put the key in the door of his car. He wondered why he had locked it; nothing ever got stolen in Stanton. They began shoving each other, and as Richard started his car Tommy

169

picked up Hollins and threw him down in the newly planted flowers in front of the 7-Eleven. Boyle immediately jumped on the back of Tommy, who spun him off just as quickly. Road Runner gave Boyle a violent shove and he joined Hollins in the dirt. Boyle scrambled up and Road Runner chased him around the back of the building into the dark alley. Tommy pounced on Hollins, screwing his face into the dirt. That was all Richard saw before putting the car in gear and driving away. He was sure he'd hear all about it in every way imaginable come Monday. When the other workers asked what had happened, what he had done on the trip, he'd have to tell the truth. He did what he had to do.

Acknowledgments

When the publishing gods make you wait as long as they have made me wait for my first book to be published, the list of people to thank is going to be long and varied.

Starting from the beginning, there is my first writing teacher, Tom Jenks, and fellow readers/writers Vivian Carmichael, Cinita Santana, and Mike Martin. I'd like to thank all the instructors and fellow writers and dreamers at St. Mary's, especially Lou Berney, Jervey Tervalon, Pam Houston, Thomas Cooney, Denise Simard, and Toner Mitchell.

A special thanks to Rob Haswell, who has been a great friend and reader from the very start, and I am sure will be to the very end.

Finally, this book doesn't sniff daylight without the support, guidance, and inspiration of Tamra Horton and our daughter, Hadley Rose.

ABOUT THE AUTHOR

Sam Silvas received his MFA from St. Mary's College and lives in Claremont, California, with his family. In life and in writing, he strives to be deceptively honest. This is his first book.

Made in the USA
San Bernardino, CA
27 February 2017